DAEMON'S KISS

ATIERNAN BOOK TWO: DAEMON BLADE SERIES

LANA SKY

Daemon's Kiss

Daemon's Kiss By Lana Sky

———)⟶•

Copyright © 2022 by Lana Sky
All rights reserved.

No part of this publication may be reproduced, distributed, or transmitted in any form or by any means, including photocopying, recording, or other electronic or mechanical methods, without the prior written permission of the author.

This is a work of fiction. Names, characters, businesses, places, events and incidents are either the products of the author's imagination or used in a fictitious manner. Any resemblance to actual persons, living or dead, or actual events is purely coincidental.

Cover Design and Interior Formatting by Charity Chimni
Editing by Charity Chimni

Acknowledgments

Thanks so much to everyone who supported this draft along the way, including the many beta readers who provided encouragement! Please keep in mind that this story includes dark, graphic, and explicit content matter that may not be suitable for readers under the age of 18—or for readers who are uncomfortable with the following subject matter: age-gap relationships, explicit sex, and graphic depictions of violence.

"Please, for the love of whatever God you pray to, try not to get blood on my floor," a gruff voice commanded. "I just waxed it. And I hope it goes without saying that using magic here, out in the open, is a no-go. I don't have the resources to memory wipe a score of mortals. I just hope no one saw you appear out of thin air."

After days spent in Atiernan's protected corner of the world, Miranda had forgotten what it felt like to be a part of the painfully modern, bustling reality most mortals lived in these days. There was more to it than electricity and advanced devices.

Most people—mortal and daemon alike—had such a blunt way of discourse apart from the rich, coded language Atiernan and his ilk preferred. More jarring than the realization that she had somehow traversed two realms in an instant, was hearing someone speak of magic so openly.

Especially when they shared such a striking resemblance to her former captor. Feeling dizzy, she inspected the man in question from over her shoulder. His dark hair and eyes were the main features that set him apart from Atiernan, the daemon lord. Otherwise, they could have been twins.

Or father and son.

"There is one reason why I haven't killed you," Marcus explained, sitting across from her at a polished wooden table. After ushering her inside, seemingly through the back door, he'd led her here—a spacious, clean area that she couldn't name the purpose of right away. A dining room?

"Can you guess what that might be?"

"Where are we?" Miranda demanded.

Not in a dungeon, at least. In any case, it seemed worlds apart from Atiernan's lavish, gothic-style manor. The walls were paneled wood, the same color as the table, which sported a metal napkin holder and a dispenser of plastic silverware—several identical tables filled the spacious room. The sight recalled a long-lost memory.

She hadn't gotten out much before her abduction, and only while under the strictest of surveillance by one of her mother's peons. During her early childhood, she'd left the forest with a group of witches traveling to a nearby field to harvest vegetables. Afterward, they had stopped at a diner for the youngest girls to use the restroom. Though, the furniture there had been a bright vinyl instead of dark wood, both establishments sported the same cozy aura.

"This is my place," Marcus said gruffly, proving himself far more evasive than Atiernan preferred to be. "Now, this is the part where you tell me how the hell you got here."

Miranda sighed, unsure where to begin. In essence, the answer was simple—she had teleported to the mortal realm by drawing her own blood and using it as the basis for a spell impossible to craft by any other means.

Blood magic.

To his credit, she sensed that Marcus might have suspected as much. He'd bandaged her arm already, wrapping it in a length of clean gauze to staunch the bleeding. That act of kindness alone said more about him than any words could —few men would keep first-aid supplies so readily in reach.

He was used to violence. Given his apparent talent for breaching manors in Hell, she could only imagine what else he got up to in his spare time.

"You live in the mortal world," she said, rather than answer him. Viewed through a large window, the sky was a beautiful blue, and sunlight fell over the sleepy street beyond. There were no bars on the windows, and any passersby seemed more than willing to walk by this building without any visible signs of disgust.

Not only did he live in this realm, but he lived among mortal humans, with no witches or daemons in sight.

The fact confounded her. His life seemed to be a relatively comfortable one, not confined to a cage or tucked away in some forgotten corner of a coven, forever shunned until the time came to fulfill his purpose.

"I do," he said warily. "And at first, I assumed you were stalling, giving your cohorts time to catch up. Now, I think the truth is far more serious—you're in shock. How much blood have you lost? Those wounds don't seem very deep —" He nodded to her wrist, which she promptly shoved behind her back.

Shock. Miranda scoffed. What a dramatic term for a mental state more akin to abject loathing and disgust. While physically, the observation made sense—she was shivering, her teeth chattering audibly—she deserved to suffer far worse for what she'd done.

After swearing never to do so again, she had used blood magic. It was her fault—she'd let herself become too accustomed to Atiernan's strange mixture of kindness and mocking. For a brief moment, she'd let her guard down.

And when the daemons revealed their intentions to contain her, she let fear goad her into doing the unthinkable.

"Tell me what happened," Marcus suggested, changing tack. "I think I can guess how you got here. But why?" His level tone prompted her to speak without thinking.

"I never…" She eyed her bandage, noting droplets of scarlet were already seeping through the ivory material. The sight triggered tears she couldn't keep at bay. They fell silently, dripping onto the table. "Never. I'm always stronger than… I'm never weak. I never use it on my own, never."

"Blood magic," Marcus said softly, confirming her suspicion. "You used it to find me."

She scanned the room again, spying a bar and menus and another window revealing part of a quaint, small-town street. With her gaze on it, she could only shrug.

"It doesn't matter. I should go back." If Atiernan realized her absence, the bastard would rush to retaliate. In fact, she wondered if that had been his main goal—trick her into breaking their bargain first to save him the trouble of upholding his end.

Well, the daemon lord had another thing coming if he thought to evade her so easily.

"You should eat," Marcus replied, rising to his feet. He gestured to a small sandwich on a paper plate hiding behind the napkin dispenser. "And get some sleep. You need to restore your strength before you can think of going anywhere. Besides, I'm sure they wouldn't expect you to return quickly. Magic strong enough to teleport between realms usually requires the sacrifice of a limb, let alone a few drops—"

"You know what I am," Miranda croaked, clutching her injured arm to her chest. "That wasn't real, honest magic. That was corruption. I deserve to lose far more than a limb."

Marcus frowned, but she couldn't tell exactly what he thought. His eyes were hard to read, heavy lidded and averted from hers.

"Either way, your current circumstances remain unchanged. You need sleep," he insisted firmly. "My apartment is upstairs. You can use my bed. Then we'll talk about why you're here and how to get you back."

"And that's it?" Miranda asked skeptically. "You let me stay, even though I used twisted magic to find you? You have no idea what my intentions are."

"Ah, but you're wrong." He shook his head, and a low, gruff note crept into his tone. "I already told you. There is one reason why I haven't killed you yet—you were able to enter this building unscathed—" He extended his arms to imply the room around them. "Believe me, if you wanted to so much as steal one of my baby hairs, you wouldn't be sitting here right now. This place is protected far more securely than that compound you came from. Now, sleep."

There didn't seem to be any point in arguing. Marcus seemed like Atiernan in yet one more way—both men could see through someone like no other.

Her especially.

⸻⟩⸺

ONE FLIGHT of stairs led to Marcus' apartment, accessed from a back hallway, near a kitchen that was surprisingly similar to any found in Hazel's Way.

Despite resting on a surprisingly comfortable mattress, she couldn't sleep. Her mind continued to race, giving her no respite from the fears weighing on it. Here in the mortal realm, her coven was but one teleportation spell away—and for once, Hazel's Forest was the furthest thing from her mind.

She needed to get back to Hell. Face Atiernan. Get the light wood tree.

Then return to Hazel's Way with some shred of honor restored.

That mantra was all she had, and she clung to it. Eventually, she gave up trying to sleep at all and began to pace, puzzling out what logical spell might be able to help her return.

There wasn't one.

"This isn't what I meant by get some rest," Marcus remarked from the doorway of his bedroom. She wasn't sure how long he'd stood there, but his size made the space feel infinitely smaller.

While cramped, the room itself was simply furnished. Miranda had to admit that even her dungeon cell had more personal charm. Ironically, it was yet one more similarity between him and the man he claimed to be his father.

They put little stock in personal mementos.

"How have you lived this long?" she asked him, forsaking niceties. "I've heard that daemons gain their long lives from the number of souls they steal."

However, a glance at him revealed no fangs peeking beneath his upper lip.

"I wouldn't call twenty-eight particularly long," Marcus replied, crossing his arms. The movement allowed her to view the large knife tucked into his pants pocket with an ornate, black hilt. "You don't look much younger, so I'm sure you'd agree."

Her eyes bulged. They were the same exact age. "How? If you are Atiernan's son—"

"My mother has mastered various, as you would say, 'corrupted,' magics. I don't know which one she used to arrange my birth. Frankly, I don't care to. What I am sure of is that the daemon Atiernan is my sire."

A fact that he didn't seem proud to acknowledge.

Miranda could only shake her head in confusion. Even blood magic wouldn't be able to preserve a child—a living one at that—throughout the centuries. "How?"

"Was he your sire too?" he asked, avoiding the question. "Atiernan."

Miranda flinched. "No… It—he was another daemon."

A monster she couldn't even bear to apply the term father to. Merely the creature who supplied the seed required to give her life.

"I need to speak to Atiernan directly," Marcus went on, his tone serious. "My mother is planning something, and she seems to want him dead very much. I need to know why that is."

Once again, Miranda felt her eyes widen. "Liva is alive?"

Marcus chuckled. "I'm just as disappointed by that fact as you seem to be."

"You mean that you aren't in contact with her?"

"No, and I prefer not to be." A darkness fell over his expression, strengthening his resemblance to a certain daemon lord. "To her, we are not children, but tools. I would rather not play a role in her scheme, whatever it may be."

"We? Do you have siblings?"

That was one burden the universe had spared her from—no other cursed siblings to fear for. None that she knew of, at least.

"That doesn't matter right now. What's important is that you're trembling. Sweating. You also have a fever, most likely. I may not be well versed in magic, but I know the signs of some poisons. That is a nasty one flooding your system," Marcus said, once again ignoring a direct question. "I'm sure you realize it. Something that strong would require an antidote, which I don't have access to."

Miranda sighed. "I know."

She'd just ignored the signs—far more than "shock" was responsible for why she was swaying on her feet, barely able to see straight. For now, the toxin in her veins mainly caused a dull throbbing in her muscles, but soon the effects would paralyze her body from the inside out. One method of ingestion for such a poison? A steaming cup of tea, provided by a cunning mage.

Not that Miranda blamed Peony one bit. Of course, the daemon would have a failsafe. She cherished her loved one's safety and would ensure no one could threaten them for very long.

Not even witches armed with daemon magic that her lord chose to lock within a stone crypt for the hell of it.

"I think you have roughly ten hours, at most, before it runs its course," Marcus added. "Blood magic won't help you there. Returning to Atiernan's fortress, on the other hand—"

"No," Miranda spat. "I'd rather die than use it again. I can't."

"My skills aren't as vast as yours," Marcus admitted. "I could only last minutes at most in that realm before my spell lost its potency. I have yet to even see Atiernan, let alone speak to him. What you saw was merely a projection of my soul. Not a corporeal body. But you... It appears you were able to enter this realm relatively unscathed."

Miranda's cheeks flamed. "My corruption is far more insidious than yours," she spat. "Is that what you're trying to say?"

"No, not at all." Marcus raised his hands in a placating gesture. "I'm part-Raeth, remember? If anyone understands the struggle with internal corruption, it's me." She startled at his grave tone. Atiernan sometimes seemed wild when he fed. Did his alleged son experience the same?

"It's obvious that your practice as a witch has greatly enhanced what you can do with our brand of magic," Marcus continued. "The fact of the matter is, alone, I can't get you back to the fortress."

"Then you can use my blood," Miranda said, extending her arm toward him.

Marcus backed away, seemingly horrified. "No. Are you insane? A portal across the street would take too much. I wasn't kidding when I mentioned the limb. He raised his right arm, revealing a bloodied bandage wrapped from elbow to wrist. "It took four inches of flesh just for me to project myself corporeally. I can't even guarantee we could make it in one piece—"

"I need to get back," Miranda insisted. Her body might have weakened by the second, but her mind was starting to feel clearer. Only by returning to Atiernan could she retrieve a light wood tree and go home.

"I just told you why I can't help you in that department," Marcus replied.

"If you try, I'm sure you could do it. I don't even know what spell brought me here in the first place," Miranda admitted. "I don't consciously use that magic. It just…happens."

She moved past him, finding a narrow hall and, beyond it, a small kitchen with simple appliances. At random, she pulled open a drawer closest to a modest stove. Thankfully, hybrids and witches arranged their kitchens in much the same way —with the knife drawer in a similar location.

"You can form a spell strong enough to take us both to Atiernan. If you need blood, then here." She snatched a knife and brought it to her throat.

Marcus lunged, horror flashing in his gaze. "Don't!"

Miranda was faster, slicing cleanly through a vein before he could so much as flinch. The searing pain wasn't enough to keep her from choking out, "You can have it."

Atiernan had lived too damn long to wallow in pity when faced with failure. He could admit his mistakes. After all, anger was no match for shame. To be humbled by a witch not once but twice…

Hell, it served him right. He just loathed that the others were forced to suffer along with him. They deserved his full attention and support. He could punish himself later. Preferably once they were out of Liva's imminent reach.

"We're ready, my lord," Benjamin called from the center of a crowd already gathered in the great hall.

They'd sent word throughout the house to pack only what could be carried. Everything else, they would scrounge for later. As a result, several hundred panicked, fearful daemons huddled near the manor's entrance holding their most treasured belongings—and at least one weapon.

"We'll need to move quickly," Peony muttered from his side. She had a bundle of supplies slung over her shoulder.

Not far away stood Beth, sporting a similar pack. "I have already scouted out a couple of locations, but I never thought we would have to leave so soon."

"It's better than to stay," he said grimly, adjusting his grip on the sole thing of value he carried—an enchanted knife sharp enough to fell any traitorous witch to cross his path. "Let's go."

Head lowered, he led the way through the main doors and into the courtyard beyond. A blood-red sunset illuminated the long, winding path approaching the towering wall of stone forming the outer barriers. For the first time in decades, those iron gates would be thrown open. From there, they would have to make a break for the hills and pray the sentinels weren't lurking nearby. Once they made it clear of the fortress, Peony would have to fashion a portal to bring them to some other part of Hell where Liva's influence didn't reach.

The monsters weren't the only danger facing them, and the sheer depth of peril they were in plagued Atiernan's mind. Even if they made it free of the territory, who knew how long it would be before Liva came calling, her minions in tow? With Miranda cackling by her side, no doubt.

The image made him grunt, and he swore a mental promise to himself then and there. No more waiting for betrayal. As soon as he found a safe place for his pack to rest, he would go after the witch himself.

Or, should he say, the half-witch hybrid.

"Come," Peony urged as he faltered. "We should—"

She broke off as every last one of the several hundred gathered daemons went silent. Never was his pack this alarmed. A chill ran down Atiernan's spine as he spun in search of the source of the disturbance.

Had Liva arrived already?

Someone had, shirking the outer gates to appear right in the center of the courtyard. While not a painfully-beautiful blond, another familiar witch appeared out of thin air to land crouched on the dust-covered stones. Holding her was a man Atiernan vaguely recognized but didn't know.

The bastard's reputation preceded him, though—that face belonged to the mysterious figure he suspected had breached his territory not once, but twice before.

"Hold," Atiernan demanded as several warriors came from every direction, their weapons drawn. Even as he voiced the caution, he withdrew his own knife from its sheath. Warily, he scanned the two figures, noting that neither had weapons on display.

Nor were they smirking with confidence at having brought death to his doorstep.

In fact, one of them seemed halfway to death herself.

The realization shattered his rage in a heartbeat. Not only did the witch look whiter than a sheet, but he could barely hear her pulse, swishing faintly through her veins.

"What did you do to her?" Atiernan didn't recognize his own voice as he surged forward, sheathing his weapon.

"Atiernan," Peony warned. "We should be careful—"

Too late. He was already halfway to the intruders, all thoughts of betrayal forgotten. Mainly because he knew enough of Miranda to suspect the witch would face him with her head held high should she intend to destroy him. Not like this...

Held limply in the arms of someone stronger. A part of him scoffed at the unwelcome concern rising in him. Mere seconds ago, he'd been ready to gut this woman. Rip her apart. Drain her of every last drop of blood.

But someone had already tried. He didn't even need to see the wound—he could smell the blood, thick and rich.

So much damn blood.

"What happened to her?" he demanded, feeling his fangs throb in hunger. The usual haze of bloodlust didn't follow, however. Concern alone seemed strong enough to combat it.

For now.

The male daemon watched him approach in silence, but when Atiernan reached for the witch, the man relinquished her without a fight.

"What happened is you failed to intimidate me," she rasped as he pulled her close.

The raw hatred in her voice sent a fresh wave of horror washing through Atiernan, and he steeled himself for Liva to appear next. Miranda, however, didn't seem poised to deliver some villainous speech. With her head lolling against his shoulder, she seemed delirious.

"I am back for what you owe me, daemon," she croaked, her eyes finding his, glazed over with pain. "I have not breached our bargain, even if you resort to dirty tricks."

"Dirty… What are you talking about?" he asked.

Though, how she managed to speak at all? Atiernan had no idea. She was so damn pale. Her pallor after the sentinel attack seemed rosy in comparison. Whether the sickly hue was due to Peony's poison or blood loss, he couldn't tell.

No matter the cause, in his arms, she felt so damn frail. Insubstantial. One look at her from this angle revealed the source of the blood instantly—a cut in her throat, bleeding freely.

Atiernan felt his fangs fully lengthen, but the feeling washing over him wasn't the mindless craze of bloodlust. Not for *her* blood, at least.

"You—" He whipped around to face the figure watching him with soulless black eyes. "What did you do to her?"

"I didn't harm her," the daemon male said. "But she needs urgent treatment, or she'll die. She was poisoned—"

"I'll prepare an antidote," Peony said softly. "Everyone inside. It seems as if our plans have changed. Now! Enough gawking. Go!"

"Yes," Atiernan rasped amid the confused murmurs of his packmates. "We will stay for now," he declared, raising his voice. He could hear voices of discontent, but he'd deal with them later. "As for you—" He turned to the stranger. "Will you submit to being detained until I speak with you directly?"

"I can't leave here without her," the male replied. "But I make one request—your men will find a knife on me. I ask that you keep it close by. Please."

Fair enough.

"Take him to a room and guard him," Atiernan commanded his nearest guard. "Keep his knife under lock and key, but somewhere close."

"My Lord." The man hesitated, his fangs bared, eyes fixed on the newcomers. "Sir, should they be in the dungeon—"

"Don't question me," Atiernan snapped.

Admittedly, it was a dilemma he pondered himself. How convenient. Right before they could leave the fortress and risk the wilderness beyond, Miranda returned, seemingly in one piece. Yet, their problems were far from solved.

Someone had breached the perimeter wall to let another sentinel inside. All evidence still pointed to Miranda.

And her weakened state would leave her especially vulnerable to any attempt he might make to scry her mind and find the answers himself.

For now, he focused on keeping her alive—whether in spite of her injuries, or his own people who glowered as he stalked past, crossing the courtyard.

With her in his arms, he entered the manor, heading blindly into a room he vaguely recognized as his. Placed on the blood-red sheets, Miranda seemed more specter than woman. The only aspect of her that had any substance were those blazing dark eyes fixated on his.

"You fooled me, daemon," she said, her voice hoarse. "I should kill you for what you did. You promised me—"

"Don't speak." He snatched a handful of bedsheets and pressed them to the bleeding wound at the base of her throat. As always, her scent threatened to overwhelm him. Drown him.

But…

The thready pulse he could hear fighting to churn blood through her veins restrained the primal impulses.

Even the monster within him didn't want her dead. Not yet. He preferred this body in full health, able to supply blood for as long as he pleased to sample it.

But that meant keeping her alive, a task that seemed monumental once her wound was taken into account. *Damn.* Atiernan hissed through his teeth, unable to ignore an inevitable outcome broadcasted by her feathering pulse and slowed breathing. One didn't need to be a warrior to sense the threat of death in the air.

"Heal yourself," he commanded, facing her. "I know you can."

Stubbornly, she eyed the ceiling, devoid of her rage in favor of shame. "Witches cannot—"

"You are no witch," he snarled over her. "I know what you are, so you can drop the act. Though I must admit that I'm surprised your coven allowed your kind on their precious lands. You must have fooled them well."

Her expression shifted, but not in the way he expected. Rather than smug, she looked…

Devastated. As if he'd mortally wounded her in a way more damaging than a lethal poison or freely-bleeding cut.

A reply sprung from his lips instinctively before he could even think it through, "I'm sorry—"

"I am a *witch*," she said coldly. "Whether you or anyone else take issue with that doesn't matter to me. I am a daughter of Hazel's Way. Nothing less. Nothing more."

He frowned. When Peony first revealed her heritage, he hadn't believed it. Not until he saw her reaction for himself. She was a half-breed, alright. Suddenly, so much about this infuriating woman began to make more sense.

"Those marks on your arms—" He was alarmed to find she sported new ones, crudely wrapped in stained bandages. "Were they created via blood magic?"

If so, that made her an enemy more dangerous than even Liva. The latter required victims—willing and otherwise— to fund her wicked dark art. A powerful witch armed with her own supply of daemon blood would be…

Unstoppable.

"You knew," she accused with a harsh laugh. Sweaty and pale, she looked far from dangerous. He felt compelled to move closer, but not because he feared she'd try to escape.

She looked more liable to fall if he wasn't there to catch her. Hold her. Do *something.* Within a few seconds, he found himself sitting beside her in an awkward compromise, his back to the headboard, still holding a wad of fabric to her throat.

"Knew what?" he responded absently to her accusation.

She angled her face away from him. "What I am. It's why you had me restrained in the first place. In the dark. You knew. Did my mother tell you all about how to make me comply—"

"I never told anyone to harm you, let alone lock you in a crypt," he snarled, angrier at the accusation than he'd been at her supposed betrayal. "Never. In your anger, you leave and bring back a daemon. For what? To destroy us all?"

"Of course not." She rolled over to face him, and he was unnerved to find that genuine alarm had displaced her anger, rendering her expression blank. She wasn't lying. "I came back to fulfill *our* bargain. Your business with Marcus is your business."

He scoffed. "It isn't like you to play semantics, Miranda. *Marcus.* Who is he? Your lover? Do you aim to conspire with Liva and lead her and her horde of sentinels to my doorstep?"

He waited for a denial. Instead, she replied by raising an eyebrow—though even that seemed to require much of her strength. She winced and went limp again, her skin glossy with sweat.

"Is this your idea of torture, daemon?" she whispered. "Let me bleed out as you pepper me with pointless questions? I think I prefer the crypt."

Her visible shudder undermined that boast.

"No." He lifted the handful of sheets from her throat, unsurprised to find her blood still flowing. A wound that deep would need far more than stitches. Only magic, perhaps. "You need healing. Can your Marcus do so?"

She attempted to shake her head but gave up with a wince. "I doubt it. He isn't skilled in magic."

"Then Peony?"

Her arm twitched in a way that might have been a shrug. "I don't know."

"Heal yourself then," he growled, increasingly exasperated by her seeming lack of concern toward her own mortality. "You can do so. Witch magic or not."

Though did he truly want to witness her use blood magic before him? Either way, she hissed at the idea.

"No." Her eyes blazed with renewed stubbornness. "I'd rather die."

"And forsake your precious tree?" he countered. Did that totem still hold any importance to her?

Oh yes. He could see the desire flickering in her eyes. She was tempted, but nowhere near enough to act. "I can't…"

"Then, if you are a daemon, daemon blood should be enough to heal you," Atiernan suspected. *No,* a part of him snarled. *Have you lost your damn mind?* How many years had he sworn never to give so much as a drop of his saliva to a witch, let alone blood? Admittedly, the plan wasn't ideal.

But it might have been Miranda's only hope—an option only viable due to her half-daemon nature. Unless he felt like hunting down Peony before the witch bled out, they had no other choice. At least via this method, she would no longer require an antidote—his blood alone would more than suffice.

Newly convinced, Atiernan met her gaze. "You must feed from me—"

"No!" She mustered her strength to lift her head, and he knew she would run if she could. Prepared to stop her, he shifted, leaving his hands at the ready. A part of him warned how useless any refusal on her part would be. Pinning her down and shoving his blood into her mouth would be child's play. She couldn't resist.

But he sensed that if he did so, it would be no different than forcing himself on her. She would feel just as violated in the end.

And a sudden explanation for her disgust toward blood magic came to mind—one that had nothing to do with haughty witch sensibilities. "Those times you used blood magic… They weren't for your own gain," he surmised. "You had no choice."

Her expression told him more than enough, and he hissed in what might have been sympathy. The cruelty… The madness… He'd believed witches, who so prized their purity, would be above such sin.

Apparently, every race had its weaknesses, and power tended to be at the root of it.

"They made you use it," he decided, confident that he'd hit the nail on its head. "And you would refuse. So, they locked you in the dark and weaponized your fear until you complied. By the time you finally broke, you'd be desperate enough to claw open your own flesh with your nails or teeth. Over and over, they did this to you."

And yet she was willing to go to the ends of the earth for a fucking tree prized by their kind.

"You have no right to judge us," she rasped, revealing where her loyalties still lay.

With that damn coven.

"They took from you, Miranda," he replied, willing to pivot to a different tack. "In a way, no one, daemon, witch, or mortal should ever be abused. But I'm not aiming to do the same."

He tugged her closer, propping her head in the crook of his arm. In the same motion, he drew his knife and watched her eyes widen in alarm. She was too weak to do more than squirm, easily restrained. Rather than brandishing the blade in her direction, he brought it to his wrist and sliced into the flesh.

"I want to *give* to you," he said as his blood began to flow. As used to pain as he was, he barely felt the resulting sting. "You need to heal. You want that tree? Then take the strength you need to retrieve it from me. Don't tell me you'd rather give up now."

She watched him, growing paler by the second. He could almost see the war taking place in her mind. Pride over her misplaced sense of honor?

"Drink, Miranda. You'll die if you don't, and our bargain won't mean much if you cross over to the afterlife. Drink."

He brought his wound to her lips, and she shied away. "Don't—"

Apparently, kindness and mercy only went so far with her. He decided to try the one emotion she had yet to resist— pride. "You think your witch brethren would honor your death if they heard you died in the arms of a daemon?"

She flinched, her expression conflicted. Yet, Atiernan had been in more than enough battles throughout his lifetime to sense when one had been thoroughly won.

When he lowered his wrist again, her lips parted.

And, as the first drop fell onto her waiting tongue...

She swallowed.

THREE

Miranda automatically swallowed the first drops of mysterious liquid to pass her lips. As dazed as she was, she could pretend it was water washing down her throat. Not a substance far more insidious, with a flavor richer than any wine she'd tasted.

Unfortunately, few things in life could fit such a description.

One realization outweighed the identity of the mystery substance—the source. She wasn't lying entirely on a mattress, but something firm, unsettlingly warm. A surface with a heartbeat raging beneath her ear.

"Drink." The voice rumbled through her jawline, providing painful clarity as to just what she rested against. *Who*, in fact.

The owner of the arm against her lips. Gods, what was she doing? There was no escape from the act. In her right mind, she would never...

But as more liquid dripped between her lips, her stomach lurched in ravenous hunger, and there was no choice. Instinct took over, demanding more of this substance she suddenly craved more than air. More than anything.

"Drink," her captor urged, pressing his arm more firmly against her lips. Obediently, she lurched up, sealing her mouth around the edge of the shallow wound.

Then she cringed and tried to recoil. He followed the motion of her lips, however, ensuring a steady stream of fresh liquid entered her mouth. Only when she went still did he finally relent.

Even so, she hesitated to move her lips even a fraction. Despite his stoic calm, the man had to be cringing every time she swallowed. Yet, he sighed as more liquid poured down her throat.

"Good," he praised, much to her shock. His tone sounded the furthest thing from disgusted. No, if anything, he sounded…

In pleasure.

"Not so gentle," he scolded as she faltered. "Take what you need from me or waste it."

Waste. The concept was horrifying. How could anyone waste something that tasted like heaven itself? She opened her mouth wider, tilting her head back to properly suckle.

This time, she received a low grunt of approval from him. Atiernan. It was *his* arm she fed from—a thought that would have horrified her any other time.

Almost as much as drinking blood at all would. The substance had become such a twisted, taboo subject in her experience. There was no way in hell she'd willingly imbibe it, especially from a daemon.

But she had been starving, deprived of a sustenance she could only now recognize as vital. Every drop thrummed through her veins, electrifying and reinvigorating exhausted muscles and shot nerves. She needed more…

And more.

And more, still.

No! It physically hurt to pry her mouth away, but she gulped at the air instead. She wasn't some mindless beast. She could control herself. *Breathe…*

This time, Atiernan didn't stop her. "You can take more," he said, keeping his arm within her reach. "I think you've gotten enough to fully heal, at least."

She shook her head, too exhausted to move. Disgust wasn't all that held her back from taking more. Just acknowledgment. He freely gave of himself only to help her. She would take enough to do so, not a drop more.

Though she could have fed for an eternity if he'd let her.

"Thank you," she rasped, finding his gaze. "Thank you." She meant it—and that terrified her.

Atiernan lowered his wrist and fisted his fingers in the rumpled bedsheets at his hip. She sensed it was a way of occupying his hand with something—something other than touching her.

"You've never taken the blood of another before." It wasn't a question—merely a statement of curiosity, voiced without the hostility she'd come to expect.

She winced anyway. "No. I would never." Not only out of sheer disgust, either. Bloodletting was a painful, degrading process. "It hurts—"

"Not me," Atiernan countered. Her face was still against his chest, but she didn't have the strength to move. Not that he seemed in a hurry for her to. "You didn't hurt me."

"It hurts me," she admitted, closing her eyes against the wave of memories threatening to descend.

Silence, her mother would snarl over her cries. *You infernal beast. Silence!*

But the pain was always too intense for her to bear in silence, at least as a child. She'd scream her throat raw, until she could only whisper.

"Every time I... It's excruciating. As if every part of my being is rebelling against the corruption. I can't breathe. I never choose to do it, never. I just..."

Reached a breaking point, and instinct took over.

Atiernan accepted those words in silence. Opening her eyes, she couldn't bring herself to see his expression. Instead, she marveled at the strangely musical cadence of his heartbeat —slightly faster than hers.

Somehow, the sound gave her the courage to ask, "I honored our bargain. Why did you lock me away—"

"I didn't," he swore heatedly. "Believe me, I will punish who did, but now you should rest. Later, I will demand from you answers to my own questions. I suggest you enjoy this truce, witch. I don't offer them to your kind often."

It sounded like a threat, but she wasn't inclined to react with anger.

"Ask me now," she rasped. "I'm fine."

She expected to be peppered with questions regarding Liva or Marcus.

Instead, he hesitated. "Who was your father?"

It was a dangerous question. One she'd never entertain in her right mind, and if he hadn't offered her something so intimate, so freely.

He'd been right—she wasn't used to taking, just being used.

In this case, she could return the favor.

"All I know is that his name was Azareal."

"Ah." Atiernan sucked in a harsh breath. "I know the name. A Vaer daemon. He fashions himself as a deal maker to mortals, using their desperation to fulfill his twisted motives. I can guess how your mother encountered him."

In a way no honest witch would ever admit.

"The story changes every time she tells it," Miranda said softly. "Sometimes, he's a monster. Sometimes, a cruel prankster who twisted her plea for his own gain. I think the truth is far simpler. She made a deal with him for power and the ability to defeat her enemies at every turn. In the end, she got me."

Atiernan grunted in agreement, but she marveled at how calmly he seemed to accept her nature. So far, he hadn't threatened to kill her as a sacrifice to appease the gods—a step up from how most witches responded to her true heritage.

"You were raised within the coven?" he asked.

She nodded, amused at how easy it was to retell this story after years spent suppressing every sordid detail. "My mother was a skilled witch, from an influential family. Her transgression caused no end of scandal, as I'm sure you can imagine. The coven nearly split in half, with a few still leaving in protest regardless. But my mother can be cunning when she needs to be. She spun the tale as her being an innocent violated by a cruel beast, shouldered with a corrupted baby as a result. But, as damaged and twisted as I was, I still had a drop of witch's blood. To abandon me would be cruel, or so she claimed. For that reason alone, she kept me."

"And they taught you their magic?"

"No," Miranda said. That would have been a step too far— and the source of her second biggest secret. "I was never allowed within their training circles like the other young acolytes. I taught myself. Every spell and potion I've learned, was through trial and error."

He made a sound low in his throat that caught her off guard. Not pity or disbelief, but respect?

"You and Peony have far more in common than I thought. Hundreds of years of practice, and she still has much to learn. She'd be impressed to know that you were self-taught."

"I don't blame her," Miranda said. "For poisoning me. It was far more humane than any other method she could have chosen. Very clever."

"She would get a kick out of that. Praise from a witch, hybrid or not."

"She is the first I've ever practiced magic with," Miranda admitted.

And it shouldn't have been so thrilling an activity.

"It was your mother who had you use blood magic," Atiernan surmised. "She locked you in darkness until you complied."

Miranda nodded, feeling her eyes burn. "Small things at first. Enhancing her spells. Ensuring a bit of trickery would go off without a hitch. Then larger, more demented requests."

"I will not judge you," Atiernan insisted. "Anything you did was not of your own free will. You shouldn't be punished for that."

"I deserve to be punished," Miranda croaked. Her throat tightened, and she wanted to shy away from the memories like she usually did. Something in the hard contours of the body against her destroyed her pathetic resolve. There was no use in keeping these secrets any longer.

"She wanted to become crone, so she used me to ensure no one could stand in her way. If they did, they met grisly accidents that took them out of contention." Her voice broke. Gods above, it sounded so ruthless when said out loud.

Like the actions of an attack dog, not a child.

"I see." Atiernan's tone was gently neutral. "And no one realized she was using blood magic?"

Miranda shrugged. "They did, but she could refute every claim. You don't understand… Most in the coven were openly suspicious of me, but they preferred to ignore my presence altogether. My mother? She was the cruelest, using every chance to refer to my existence as evidence of the threat daemons pose to our kind. So, who could accuse my most vicious detractor of benefitting from my magic in secret?"

"That's…vile," Atiernan said, his voice rumbling. "And no one noticed the scars on your arms?"

"I wore clothing designed to hide them," she admitted, eyeing one blood-stained forearm. "Most never came close enough to notice."

"I'm sorry."

"Don't be," she hissed, horrified. "I don't need your pity."

"It isn't pity to acknowledge obvious mistreatment," he countered, adjusting his arm as if to prevent her from pulling away. "You didn't deserve that."

"I didn't?" She lifted her head to glare at him, convinced he was mocking her. Surprisingly, his expression conveyed only confusion, and she felt driven to explain, "I am an abomination, the fact that my mother even allowed me to survive my birth is a mercy I owe her my life to repay. Serving her will was the least I could do."

No matter what it cost her. No matter how much it hurt in the end.

No matter how evil each bit of magic felt.

She would honor her family and her coven, no matter the cost.

"You don't believe that," Atiernan replied, prompting her to turn away.

Damn the daemon and his seemingly earnest frown. The window across the room seemed a safer view than his expression.

"That I owe her? I do."

"No. That you are an abomination."

She frowned. Her whole outlook on the world hinged on that belief. How ironic that a daemon would be the first person to ever challenge that position.

"I am," she said softly. "A corruption of nature, unfit for life."

"And your mother?" His mouth chased her ear as she turned away again. "Is she 'fit for life' after making a deal with a daemon and using the resulting child to fund her ambition? Or the women in your precious coven who conspired to shun and ostracize you? And yet, you seem determined, not to secure your own safety, but to find some damn tree that I'm sure has no real meaning to you—"

"You're wrong." She craned her neck to meet his gaze, surprised by the anger she saw there. "That tree means everything to me. Because…"

"Why?"

"Because my birth is what destroyed it. Twenty-eight years ago, the mere second I drew my first breath, the tree ignited and was consumed by the resulting fire. What does that say if not that I am cursed? The gods were so angered by my mere existence that they punished the entire coven in return."

A shame she'd carried her entire life.

Rather than voice his agreement, the daemon… Laughed? A guttural sound rumbled through his chest, making her quiver in response. Definitely a laugh. Then came his voice, octaves deeper than before. "You blame yourself, for committing the crime of merely being born?"

"I blame the inherent wickedness my nature entails," Miranda replied. "I should have never existed."

"But you do. No, don't scoff. Look at me—" Atiernan cupped her chin, forcing her to hold his gaze. "You do exist, and if you think some burning tree discounts your right to live, then I am sorry to tell you, Miranda—you know nothing about how the world works."

"I don't? And some daemon is going to enlighten me?"

"Yes," he replied. "Don't forget that Liva brought that tree to your coven. I'm sure it was placed with countless spells for her own benefit. Such as destroying itself should it sense the presence of a daemon. Not out of some divine righteousness, but spite. You merely sprung a trap set for me."

His tone softened, as if he truly felt guilty for a lifetime of pain.

"Why?" she demanded, blinking back unwanted tears.

"Because witches aren't inherently good, and daemons aren't inherently evil," he explained. "We are all subjected to free will and able to make our own choices. Even someone as long-lived as Liva is subject to the same petty whims as someone like your mother. A person's core does not change, no matter the number of years lived."

"You've changed," she pointed out. "I've heard the stories."

Those involving a man who committed unspeakable sins. Though maybe this was his roundabout way of confirming her worst fears—his claim to be reformed was a lie. Once a heartless monster, always a heartless monster.

Although he didn't seem like much of a monster anymore. His head was tilted, his expression thoughtful.

"Some might say that who I am was always there, buried beneath the shame and anger and the hatred that drove me," he confessed, his voice low. "I will not and cannot make excuses for the atrocities I committed. I am the same person now as I was then. The difference? I can acknowledge the consequences of acting without restraint, and I do my best to keep those worst impulses in check."

His tone alluded to a deeper, internal struggle she could only fathom. Did Marcus feel the same? She recalled that he'd mentioned a similar dilemma, but her thoughts were too flimsy to grasp. She could only listen.

"You are no more an abomination than any other creature in this world," Atiernan went on. "You have just been forced to acknowledge your darker impulses far earlier than most."

"I didn't tell you the worst of it," she croaked, huddling against him. "One of those women... She was struck with an incurable illness and died because of me. Because of my blood magic."

The incident haunted her. While her mother's scorn might have played a role in her self-loathing, deep down, she knew the truth—there was plenty about her to fear, and they all couldn't be blamed on Agatha Lightwood.

"I am a monster," she rasped.

"No. You can acknowledge that sin and atone for it," Atiernan replied. "Pining for some tree or suppressing your magic doesn't fix that. Ensuring that it can never happen again will. Facing your mother and calling out her crimes, that will."

His words made her head hurt. She felt dizzy. Weightless.

"You are strange, daemon," she blurted, eyeing him through her lashes. "Pretty strange. Pretty and strange."

It wasn't fair how someone like him so effortlessly radiated beauty. From this angle, his hair and those unsettling eyes made him resemble a divine creature born of hellfire.

"I've been called worse," he said. "Mainly by other witches."

Miranda sighed. "I may be a fake witch, but I am a mortal woman through and through."

Which sadly meant, witch or not, she wasn't as resistant to his inherent male charms as she wished. Belatedly, her body seemed to realize the hard, male frame against it and reacted. Her belly flipped. Breathing became a struggle, but not because of a life-threatening wound. Just weakness.

"No one can take that away from me, daemon. I may be an abomination, but I am mortal at my core. It means nothing if I relent to your comfort, or find you attractive. Plenty of women have craved you," she added sleepily.

Therefore, no harm, no foul if her heart was racing due to his nearness.

Atiernan didn't seem to agree with her logic. "You didn't drink much, but I believe you might be blood drunk," he admonished, stroking the corner of her mouth. "You should rest."

"Will you stay with me?" The words passed her lips before she could hold them back.

And he wanted to refuse. She could tell from how his eyes cut to slits. Yet, he didn't push her off. "Do you want me to?"

His voice vibrated through her bones, deeper than ever.

"Yes," she admitted, though the answer puzzled her. It sounded way too genuine, drunkenness or not. "I want you to."

She might regret the request later, but that didn't change the present reality.

Atiernan, the daemon lord, was a welcome distraction from her thoughts—one she selfishly needed. For the first time in so long, she didn't have to endure being alone.

But, in a way, he terrified her far more than the darkness ever could.

FOUR

Common sense sounded a warning Atiernan was reluctant to hear. There were so many reasons why he should have left the witch, and perhaps regulated her to a dungeon while he was at it. When Peony knocked on the door sometime during the night, antidote in hand, he didn't take advantage of an easy way to exit, with the witch none the wiser.

Instead, he turned the mage away and remained in bed, Miranda in his arms.

Nothing was more dangerous than lying with her, enduring her sweet scent, and trying to ignore the blood drying on the sheets. Surprisingly, it was easy to control himself, as long as he focused on her obvious discomfort with blood.

And it confounded him thoroughly that she'd allowed him to feed from her before.

At least now he knew why her blood held such appeal.

She was a hybrid, endowed with the magic that flavored the blood of a witch, enhanced with her part-daemon nature. All in all, a creature plenty would kill to possess.

And for most of her life, being used as a tool was the only reality she'd known.

Anger filled him at that. He pictured the nameless crone Miranda had been cursed to call a mother , and for a second —just one—he indulged fantasies of what the man he used to be would do to such a villain.

And yet, when Miranda referred to the woman, it wasn't with hate or rage. She didn't resent her.

She hated herself.

He couldn't resist fingering a dark tendril of her hair as she slept against his chest. She could seem so daunting, endowed with the confidence that had fooled him into believing she'd been a pure-blood witch from the start. Then, in moments like this, she could seem so fragile. Delicate. One wrong move could damage her irreparably, and he felt a strange protectiveness take root.

A need to protect her from all who would do her harm.

Even from herself if he had to.

And yet, his growing respect for her aside, there were uncomfortable dilemmas to deal with. Ones her true nature brought to the surface. Peony had lied to him to protect her —he didn't doubt that. She was a dangerous risk with her sort of magic—no wonder the mage had poisoned her as a failsafe. If she were one of Liva's consorts, he might as well slit his throat now.

As well as that of everyone within his manor.

They were doomed.

Then there was the question of the man she'd brought with her. A part of him wished his concerns were strictly relegated to the risks of another daemon he didn't know—not jealousy.

Marcus. She'd referred to him by name, with a note of respect that he hadn't missed. Who was that man to her? And why had she resorted to using her blood magic to find him?

On top of many other pressing issues, he also needed to have a word with Benjamin about why he saw fit to restrain Miranda in the first place. Any other night, he'd be storming through the manor, determined to conquer every problem at once. Now?

He couldn't bring himself to move. The sight of one sleeping witch shouldn't have stirred him so much. The feel of her in his arms shouldn't have been so wonderfully alien.

He'd had enough women in his lifetime—a number that helped his centuries of celibacy seem more like a welcome break than a punishment.

Once, he thought he'd even known love, experienced with a woman he cherished above all others.

So, he knew enough to recognize that what he felt for Miranda was the makings of something nefarious. Had he any sense, he'd leave this room now and have her bound in chains.

Still, he didn't move, preferring to lean against the headboard of the bed and watch her chest rise and fall beneath her blood-splattered dress.

Objectively, there was little about her that should have appealed to him, if anything. Every glance, however, revealed more than he had initially noticed. Her eyes. The way her gaze clouded over when she was upset. How her cheeks flushed with indignant rage when she challenged him.

How she seemed unworthy within her own skin, as if she were afraid that any moment those gods she prayed to might descend from the heavens to end the life she stole.

It bothered him more than he wanted to admit, imagining the pain she'd been subjected to. As a hybrid, growing up among daemons, her life would have been hard. But among self-righteous witches who saw themselves the stewards of nature itself?

It must have been hell. One few could survive unscathed.

Why that endeared her to him more? He had no damn idea. This woman could kill him ten times over, and yet... He breathed her in and felt no urge to budge.

Finally, after hours, she stirred, murmuring sleepily. Only then did he shift to put some distance between them.

"You can leave if you want," she croaked, apparently not asleep at all. "You must have a lot to see to. I understand."

"No," he replied without an ounce of regret. "I want to stay."

Her eyes peeked at him from beneath heavy lids. "Why?"

It was a question that haunted him in more ways than one. Why had he given her his blood despite his personal vow never to do so again? Why was he so relieved by the color returning to her fragile limbs? Why were his nostrils flaring still, desperate to inhale her scent?

Ironically, all those questions and more seemed to be answered by one response.

"Because you need me."

She didn't *want* him—and that was the one fact that made him relent in every instance. She never asked for his blood. Or his protection. Of all the things he could have offered her, she asked for his presence, or a tree that held no true meaning to her.

She was so damn selfless, and her naivety made him selfish. Poor, little witch. He'd devour all of her if he could, and yet she seemed reluctant to allow herself even the smallest of mercies.

"You need me to stay, so I'll stay," he reiterated when she remained silent.

He knew she wanted to deny that.

But she didn't.

"I know what you really want," she said softly. "My blood. My body. Just take it."

"No. I don't—"

"Take what you want from me so you can leave me alone." She raised her wrist, pressing the fragile limb to his chest. "I mean it. I'm offering myself to you, so consume your fill."

"I don't want you to sacrifice yourself to me," he snapped, shrugging her off. "I want…"

Something far too dangerous to put into words.

"What?" she demanded, unsatisfied. "Tell me now, so that whatever it is, you can just take it and leave!"

"Fine." His hand latched onto the back of her skull, drawing her closer—gently. He made sure to keep every touch and movement easy enough to prevent causing her harm. His point was made all the same. Inches away, her eyes stared fearfully, her frantic breaths perfuming his skin.

"I want you to drop the martyr act," he said, feeling his fangs throb, desperate to descend. "You enjoyed the taste of my blood. Good. Take more of it. You like when I feed from you. Relish it. And when I touch you… I want you to take your pleasure and stop hiding from it. Do that, and you can have far more than one damn tree."

"I can't," she whispered. "I can't."

"You won't," he corrected, fixating on her trembling mouth. "That's the problem. You will never consciously make a choice to want me. So don't let yourself dwell in guilt and shame. Just react the way you want to. Trust your instincts for once."

Though the advice was a double-edged sword. He'd spent decades learning to control his. Every impulse demanded he take her *now*. Pin her to this bed and let his primal urges dictate what happened next. He'd spent centuries suppressing everything that made him a daemon...

How hypocritical was it to demand she do the opposite? Stop repressing and learn that there was nothing to be ashamed of by embracing her wilder instincts.

"Kiss me," he taunted. "Not now, but when you've healed. Give me that much, and I'll be satisfied."

She flinched back, shaking her head. Already, her throat had healed—even the marks from the sentinel were beginning to fade, leaving remnants of the stitches against smooth flesh. Surprisingly, only his bite marks remained—two stubborn pinpricks of angry red. "I don't want to—"

"Liar," he spat.

She gulped as if she weren't used to being called out so bluntly. Years in isolation, had anyone ever noticed the woman she'd grown into? He knew her stories of countless lovers had been a lie, but he'd felt the evidence for himself that she wasn't entirely untouched. But no one had ever looked at her with desire, not like he did. He could discern that much.

"Even if I wanted to kiss you," she said hoarsely, "I couldn't."

"Why?"

She sighed in exasperation. "Because… I should hate you. All that you are. I should hate myself for even wanting to —" She broke off, her expression horrified. "This is a game to you, daemon, but this isn't fun for me. It's…"

Excruciating. Contrary to her insistence, he did know exactly what she felt.

Gingerly, he turned to sit on the edge of the bed, his feet on the floor. With his back to her, he suggested, "Give me one last thing, and I'll go."

"What?"

"I told you once that I found you beautiful. Do you believe that?"

He looked back to find her shaking her head, that unnerving vulnerability on display once more. "No."

"Then will you let me tell you why I think so?"

She licked her lips in a motion that made him silence a groan. When she didn't answer, he took her silence as consent.

"I think you are beautiful, not because of your physical looks," he admitted. "Not entirely. You are beautiful because, though you think there is nothing about you worth desiring, you guard yourself fiercely. Deep down, you know the truth, even if you shy away from admitting it. There is something in you worthy of love. Worthy of having a man, or anyone, fight for it. Something within you I crave, and it's more than your blood. More than your sex. It's you—"

He took a risk by reaching out to her and pressed his thumb to her lower lip, feeling it part in response.

"You know deep down that you are far more than the lies fed to you would let you believe. Even a daemon can see that."

She didn't believe him. Of course not. A few pretty words would never be enough to overcome years of vicious lies and abuse. But, if he had a few more days, a few years, to say those words to her every day, then perhaps...

"I'm offering you what you want, daemon," she said, crossing her arms. With that simple motion, it seemed as though she sought to lock him out. Subconsciously, she undermined her own boast. "You can have me now. All of me. To prove some asinine point, you'd walk away?"

"Yes," he admitted, though it killed him to. "Because I want you to give yourself to me of your own free will. No bargain. No trade. No doubts. I want you to be fully aware of a power far greater than blood magic."

She frowned, eyeing the bloodied sheets beneath them both. "You should go. I appreciate you wanting to stay, but... Please go."

Without a word, he stood and entered the hall. As the door closed behind him, he wondered if he'd been a fool to leave such an offer on the table. Or, if by doing so, he'd given her a gift far more valuable than some damn tree.

THE FIRST PERSON he sought out was Benjamin. Of all places, he found the man near the dungeons, feeding from a human out in the open, for anyone to see. Atiernan felt his eyes widen in shock—Ben tended to be more modest than most when sourcing blood.

The Raeth was the noble sort who valued his self-control—which Atiernan could admit rivaled only his. Until the witch, that is.

As Atiernan drew close enough to recognize the figure leaning sensually against the warrior, he suddenly understood Ben's newfound openness.

"My lord," Sanna gasped, her green eyes sparkling as Benjamin withdrew from her wrist. "You look worn. If you require sustenance, I can—"

"Leave," Atiernan demanded before turning his focus to Benjamin. "I need a word with you."

"Of course, my lord." The man swiped the blood from his lips and stood at attention. "I hope that now the danger posed by the witch is painfully clear. We can call the tribunal today, and—"

"What made you imprison the witch?" Atiernan demanded, struggling to keep his voice level. "I know about the breach, but what evidence did you have that the witch was responsible?"

Something hopefully stronger than a hunch.

Ben blinked. "My, lord... Evidence? I, well..."

Atiernan hissed through clenched teeth. As expected, the warrior had reacted on nothing more than paranoia and suspicion. "Yet you acted on *my* authority and locked a woman in a tomb anyway. Do you know what you've done? What could have happened?"

He knew he'd raised his voice, but he found it harder to rationalize the anger surging through his veins. Sure, Ben had only done what he thought necessary—but Miranda could have done far more than leave his manor with her magic. It took everything he had in him not to tan the bastard's hide to teach him a lesson.

"From now on, I am the only one who comes near the witch without a direct order," Atiernan growled instead. "Touch her again, and you will suffer for it."

"My lord?" Benjamin blinked, and a wayward drop of blood dribbled down his chin. "I don't understand."

Good. Neither did Atiernan. All he did know was a gnawing sense of unease as he walked away, leaving the stunned warrior behind.

Miranda would make for a fitting source of all the dangers plaguing them—the sentinel attacks and the breaches. Too fitting. In fact, someone seemed determined to throw all suspicion in her direction.

The potential explanations plagued him. Of course, the most obvious was that the witch was evil after all, determined to cause them harm.

Or…

There was another culprit. Either way, he planned on solving this mystery soon enough. Right after he dealt with the next issue on his list.

After making a few inquiries with the rest of his men, he learned that they put the male daemon, of all places, in Peony's storeroom—and he was sure the mage herself played no small role in arranging such accommodations. She wanted to speak to him alone, away from prying eyes. Why?

"You are sure?" Her voice drifted into the hall, and Atiernan slowed his steps to listen. "…no contact with her—"

"No," the male replied. His voice was deep, betraying no hints of an accent that alluded to him being from the daemon realm. He spoke a mortal language, English. Much like Miranda. "I haven't seen her since I was a child, and I would prefer to keep it that way."

"You expect me to believe that?" Peony's voice took on a hard edge. "How can we be sure you aren't an agent of hers?"

"An agent of who?" Atiernan raised his voice, entering the room.

Peony stood near the doorway, while the daemon sat on a chair amid a circle of black sand that he figured was enchanted. Trust Peony to take no risks. He was grateful for her vigilance, though she'd nearly killed Miranda by taking such precautions.

"An agent of Liva," the man said, meeting his gaze. "I am not. There are ways I could prove it, but most are time-consuming. The simplest is that you take my word that Liva is the last person I would ever conspire with."

"But you know her," Atiernan surmised, eying the man from head to toe.

He was stocky, with long dark hair and flashing eyes. At a glance, it was unclear whether he was mortal or daemon. His features were vague enough to belong to either race. Though, given that he still sported droplets of Miranda's blood on his face, Atiernan suspected he was familiar with dark magic in more ways than one.

"I know her," the man admitted. "Though, I wouldn't say our relationship is exactly cordial."

"What is your name?" Atiernan demanded, advancing toward him.

"Marcus."

So, Miranda knew him enough to refer to him by name with no mocking insult woven in. Was that jealousy he felt stabbing through his chest?

"Are you a daemon? How do you know the witch, Miranda?"

"She contacted me a few days ago," Marcus replied, leaning back in his chair. "Mentally. Then she used blood magic to find me in the mortal realm."

Atiernan felt his eyes widen. "You mean you lured her to you," he replied. "A lone witch can't amass that kind of magic, even a half daemon."

Though, apparently, one could. He'd seen their arrival for himself—only magic could explain it. Miranda was quickly becoming more intriguing by the second.

And more dangerous.

"She did," Marcus countered.

"You didn't answer my first question. What are you?"

The man raised an eyebrow. "You don't know who I am, do you?"

Atiernan frowned. He didn't like the meaningful glance the man sent his way. As if he were the last to grasp the punchline of some amusing joke. He especially didn't like how the man's eyes cut to Peony.

"You don't seem to be in a hurry to tell me. Should I assume you are an agent of Liva after all?"

"No," Marcus said with a low, unsettling laugh. "Not in the sense you seem to think. But I am connected to the woman in a personal sense."

"How?"

As a lover?

"She is my mother," Marcus said. "And as far as I know, *you* are my father."

FIVE

Miranda slept for too long. How she managed to in the first place, she figured she would never understand. Her body felt too languid—her first warning sign that something was horribly wrong.

The second was the sweet, haunting taste lingering on her tongue. She felt her throat work to swallow as if desperate for every last trace of the substance, whatever it was. Her brain sluggishly tried to identify it.

Not wine, or some other drink.

Not fruit, either.

Something decadent, though liquid…

No! Her eyes flew open as a horrible realization came to mind. She was tasting blood. The blood of a daemon.

She lurched upright, blinking against a stream of blazing sunlight. It seemed such a stark contrast to the chaos of the previous day, when she'd used blood magic to teleport to the mortal realm.

Only to bring back the son Atiernan had no idea existed.

She couldn't worry about that now. The man knew what she was. Only the gods knew what assumptions he'd come to after what happened between them. She needed to find him and explain.

After she cleaned up his blood *and* hers.

A groan escaped as she took in the mess splattered all over the bedsheets. She stripped them and scoured the room for a rag to clean the floors. Only then did she test the doorknob, fully expecting to find it locked. When it wasn't, she braced herself to discover a guard lurking outside it.

The figure she did find, slender and lithe, was most likely not who Atiernan would put in charge of keeping her contained.

"You're awake," the girl said softly, raising a mug she held in one hand. In the other was a pile of folded clothing. "I brought you tea. And my mother wanted me to give you one of her dresses to wear."

"I'm not thirsty," Miranda croaked, accepting the garment. Then she stood aside to allow the girl inside her room.

"Your name is Bethaem," she said, wracking her brain to remember. "Peony's daughter."

The girl shrugged and moved to place her mug on an end table beside the bed. "I prefer Beth."

Displaying nervous energy, she sat on the bare mattress, folding her hands neatly on her lap. Despite the apparent upheaval at the compound, she looked clean, and wore a gray dress, her hair neatly plaited. Her eyes, however, were bloodshot.

"I heard them talking," she said cautiously, eyeing the floor. "About you. That you are…"

Good gods. Miranda steeled herself for the typical insults —*an abomination, a freak, corrupted.*

"Like me."

"W-What?" Miranda did a double take, only belatedly remembering to school her expression. She knew firsthand the stigma of being a hybrid—and that it was better not to gape at someone revealing such a personal detail. "I… I don't understand."

She pictured the mage and wondered if she'd pegged the woman all wrong. Peony was hungry for knowledge, but hungry enough to solicit a witch for a hybrid child in return?

"My dad isn't a daemon," Beth explained. "He isn't a normal human either, or a witch. Not really. He refers to himself as a mage of sorts. He taught my mother some of what she knows about magic. When they could tolerate being in the same realm, that is."

Miranda bit her lip to hide her shock. No wonder Peony had seen right through her act. And yet, if her daughter was a half-breed, no one would know from how the rest of the daemons interacted with her. She played with the other children, and freely roamed the manor. She didn't seem isolated or despised.

Far different from the discrimination she'd been subjected to growing up in Hazel's Way.

"I… I didn't know."

"My mother says it's dangerous out there for me," Beth went on, shrugging her narrow shoulders. "It's why she keeps me here under lock and key. I mean, I'm almost seventeen, and I've never seen the mortal world. My dad wants to take me traveling with him, but if my mother has her way, I won't ever leave this place. What is it like out there? What was it like for you?"

"It was different," Miranda admitted. "I think I would have preferred to grow up here."

Accepted and cherished, unaware of the stigma she might face just because of her heritage. Beth seemed so… Normal. A glance at her bare arms revealed no scars, no attempts to use blood magic. Did the girl even know how?

"Why did you want to talk to me?" Miranda asked softly.

Beth finally met her gaze, her brown eyes comically wide. "Because you know what it's like! I've never met someone like us before, and my mother—I can't talk to her about anything. Dad is always off on his travels, but… I always thought I was a freak. But you…"

Again, Miranda prepared herself for the worst. *You're an evil bitch, so my future can't be that bleak.*

"You're powerful. Even mother is in awe of you, and I've never seen her respect anyone but Atiernan. And you can travel between the realms whenever you want. I want to be like that, too. I want to live in the mortal realm and learn magic. Maybe then my mother won't be so—"

"You don't want to be like me," Miranda croaked. When she tallied up the countless hours she used to spend wishing she'd been born a full-blooded witch… It seemed like a cruel joke that someone could aspire to suffer the same fate.

"I don't want to be in a cage for the rest of my life," Beth insisted. "I love my mother, but I can't be her perfect doll forever. Please, can you teach me? I want to learn powerful magic, like healing, and how you know about the herbs. Can you?"

"I don't know," Miranda croaked. Did she even have it in her to teach someone else? Was she worthy of doing so?

No.

But she found a nicer way of stalling. "You'd have to ask your mother, and Atiernan," she added, picturing how the daemon lord might react should he find her teaching spells to his young ward.

"I will!" Undeterred, Beth lurched to her feet. "I'll beg them until they say yes!"

She raced for the door, and Miranda could only watch her skip into the hall.

Alone, she felt more confused than ever. Unsurprisingly, one person lurked at the center of her thoughts.

Atiernan.

She needed to see him. Needed to… Question him. Erase whatever pathetic hope he'd sparked in her and remind herself how he saw her first and foremost. As an enemy. A monster. A liar.

Once bathed and dressed, she crept into the hall again, alarmed to find that no guard appeared to shadow her every move. Had he forgotten to assign one to her?

No. The back of her neck prickled with the telltale warning that she was being followed, though her pursuer remained unseen.

Or was this yet another mind game devised by Atiernan and Peony to test her loyalty? If so, she should have gladly failed. It unnerved her how readily she'd complied with their rules and requests. Playing with potions. Drinking blood. A real witch would have put up a fight. Resisted. Die rather than obey.

Some way or another, she would have to turn the tide.

To start with, she would demand Atiernan reveal exactly what he expected from her. No way in hell would she allow him to grant what she desired out of pity. She would earn every branch and leaf, even if it killed her.

Never, would she agree to take charity from a daemon.

As if the thoughts alone conjured him, she rounded a corner to find him standing there, his body rigid.

Miranda swallowed and nearly lost her resolve. For a second, she considered running. Damn her pride—Atiernan could take whatever he wished as long as he left her soul intact.

"Running to meet your cohort?" he asked, his voice dangerously low.

Uh-oh. Miranda flinched, and suddenly she wasn't in the position to make any demands of the daemon. Overnight, their dynamic had reverted to the very first day he met her in the dungeon.

Captor and captive.

Even so, she was surprised to find that she wasn't afraid only for herself. "Marcus," she croaked. "Is he alright?"

"I'm sure you'd love to know," Atiernan countered dryly. His hands were open at his sides, fingers flexing. The stance was far more aggressive than the way he'd approached even after she'd teleported into the heart of his fortress. "Was this your grand plan to undermine me?"

He advanced in a predatory way that made her entire body quiver. She jumped back.

"W-What's wrong?"

He surged forward. "I know who he claims to be," Atiernan said harshly, his eyes so cold. "Did you put him up to it? That twisted lie?"

"No," she rasped. "But I believe him."

"You do?" He cocked his head in a way that made her breath catch. With every step he took, she scrambled back two, eventually winding up with her back to the wall and nowhere to go. "And why is that? Because you planted the idea in his head?"

"N-No—" She broke off as he reached past her, gripping a doorknob to a room she hadn't noticed.

He opened it, herding her inside. Like a shadow, he crept in after her, closing the door behind them. With what she suspected was deliberate slowness, he engaged the lock.

"And why is that? Because we both are fools in the games of witches?"

"No," she rasped. "Because you both… Were kind to me."

She didn't know what he expected her to say, but her actual reaction seemed to floor him. He winced, his eyes losing their cold hue.

"Explain."

She swallowed and smoothed a hand along the skirt of her dress. "You spoke to me with respect. An infuriating quality that I assume must be hereditary."

"And this is phase two of your scheme," he suspected. "Lull me into a false sense of security, distract me with such a pathetic lie. Let me guess. Liva is lurking beyond the outer walls, waiting for her cue to strike?"

"I don't know, and I don't care," Miranda replied. "What I do care about is this. I will never be beholden to a daemon, ever. Anything you give me will be met with payment, whether it be your blood or the light wood tree. I do not want your charity."

"Oh?" Instantly, his icy demeanor returned in full. It was a miracle she didn't shiver. "So, what exactly do you offer?"

She swallowed hard before fingering the neckline of her dress. Then, she gathered the skirt and lifted it over her head. "Everything," she said breathlessly, balling the material in both hands before tossing it at his feet. "So, take your fill, because no one will ever be able to say I accepted pity from a daemon."

SIX

Atiernan didn't know whether to chalk up the woman's brazenness to delirium or sheer stupidity. Her mistake, either way—he was done playing games with Miranda Lightwood.

She wanted to be used? Abused? Violated?

He would gladly take every last drop she had to offer.

And more.

Even as the predatory thought crossed his mind, a newer sentiment replaced it.

"No. You *desire* brutality," he told her. Then he stooped for her dress and threw it at her. "You long to be able to say you endured the torture inflicted by a daemon and kept your head held high like a good little witch. So, no. I will not give you that."

He pivoted to face her, amused that she'd already dressed again. So eager was the witch to make boasts she had no intention of following through on.

What was the harm in toying with her, just a little?

Without warning, he reached out, pulling her closer, pressing his lips to hers. Rather than ravish, he restrained himself with the kiss, only going as far as she allowed him.

The gentleness shocked her, and as a result, she reacted on impulse, opening her mouth to let him in.

Giving him exactly what he wanted.

He wouldn't let her tolerate his touch like a broken captive. He'd make her work for every drop of blood he took.

He wasn't going to break her.

Miranda Lightwood would beg for this destruction.

"On your knees," he commanded, withdrawing from her parted lips. She rushed to obey, but he felt the need to issue another order. "But you keep those eyes on me."

No more hanging her head in shame.

To his shock, she complied without hesitation, brandishing that haughty chin. It seemed the witch preferred to be degraded. She liked playing the good captive.

And he was more than willing to oblige.

"I won't fuck you," he said to preface what he had in mind. Though visibly healed, the aftereffects of his blood could still be impacting her judgment. That didn't mean he couldn't taunt her.

Lip curling into a cold smile, he raked his gaze along her front. "I'm sure even witches know how to use their pretty lips in ways other than spinning lies," he suggested, hardly recognizing his voice.

Her cheeks flamed. She knew alright, and he expected her to put on a good show by refusing. His grin widened at the thought of the indignant little rant that might follow.

Instead, she settled onto her knees and reached for his slacks.

He sucked in a breath, unprepared for the heat that rose at the sight of those slim fingers extending toward his abdomen.

Damn her.

His cock throbbed, threatening to burst through the thin barrier separating him from those delicate fingers.

"I want to add another request to our bargain," Miranda added, oblivious to how his body had reacted to her approach.

Good. An evil demand, no doubt. "What would that be?"

"Beth wants to learn magic. I don't think Peony will let her, but she shouldn't be punished because of me."

He grimaced, skeptical. "And that is what you want? Me to intervene between a mother and daughter on the whims of a witch?"

It sounded insidious when said out loud. Something Liva might devise to recruit a young acolyte into her schemes. Beth was intelligent, but naïve. As far as he knew, Peony had never let her leave the fortress grounds.

With her hybrid blood—though far less powerful than Miranda's—she would make for a useful peon. He might have believed that was the witch's true aim, if it weren't for her expression. Her eyes were wide, partially visible through her lashes. The emotion glinting in them wasn't devious or prideful.

Just earnest.

Damn her.

"Enough talk," he said harshly, gesturing toward his front. "Open that mouth and put it to another use."

He expected her to balk. Instead, she fingered the fastening of his pants, undoing it expertly.

Were she any other woman, he'd cut the foreplay and move to the main event. He didn't enjoy slow buildup during mating. Just the act itself. Completion. Satiation.

Miranda wouldn't receive such mercy.

"You can't use your mouth on me if I'm fully clothed, witch," he taunted as she took her time, her hand still on his hips.

She winced, her fingers shaking. Oh, how badly she wished to maintain her confident demeanor. That appealed to him but not in the way he wanted it to.

Rather than gloat, he felt a pinch of something that might have been guilt.

"Perhaps, I should take pity on you, witch? Go back to your room—"

"No." She inhaled raggedly, her gaze meeting his. "You want me to use my mouth on you, daemon? Then hush and let me do it."

Before he could offer her another way out, she curled her fingers around the waistband of his pants and pulled, baring him to her completely.

SEVEN

Miranda wasn't quite the innocent Atiernan seemed to think she was. She had experienced sex before, though not something as degrading as fellatio. In any case, she certainly knew what the male anatomy looked like beneath clothing.

Or, at least, she thought she did.

To compare Atiernan to the bastard who deflowered her would be an insult even the daemon lord didn't deserve.

The sight of him didn't inspire the same crippling mixture of dread and revulsion. The man resembled an artwork chiseled from stone, composed of solid muscle and glorious, flawless precision.

He was beautiful.

Powerful.

Intimidating as hell.

Strength in physical form.

And she somehow had to please him using her limited knowledge of sex.

At least he had given one clue in what he expected—her mouth on him. As if that alone could work. Still, she would rather try than admit defeat.

Fighting to keep her hand from trembling, she reached for him.

"No."

His tone made her suck in a breath and wrench her hand back, but anger wasn't what she saw unfurl across that impassive expression. This was something far worse —amusement.

"I don't wish to be manhandled, witch. You've never touched a cock before, have you?"

Her face heated. She could barely maintain eye contact without cringing. "I told you that I have experienced many—"

"A lie," he bit back. "An easily disproven one, at that. You could barely tolerate my fingers inside of you, let alone multiple men. Be honest with me. What is the true number?"

She swallowed hard, desperate to maintain the lie. He *wanted* her to—she could see it in his gaze. He craved for a moment to strike and reveal her to be the naïve innocent he could gladly exploit.

"One," she admitted hoarsely. "One man, and I never touched the organ he invaded my body with. Happy?"

He wasn't. His gaze clouded over with an intensity that made her tense. Had she said the wrong thing? In a sense, yes. Perhaps Atiernan had entertained himself with thoughts of her being a virgin he could conquer.

"I'm sorry if that disappoints you, daemon—"

"Tell me how it happened," he demanded.

She stammered. "What do you mean how? I'm sure a man as experienced as you knows how it works between a man and a woman." She sneered.

He didn't even crack a smile in return. Something else weighed on his mind, troubling him to the point that he didn't even care to mock her over it. "Did he… Did he force you?"

Ah. She flinched and looked away, eyeing the bed instead. "No," she croaked. "I am not so pathetic that I lacked autonomy in every aspect of my life—"

"That's not what I meant." He was closer. His fingers cradled the side of her jaw, and she couldn't stop herself from cringing away. Rather than chase the contact, he kept his hand still, inches from her face. "Look at me, woman."

His eyes blazed when she finally did. A peek below his waist revealed that his pants were still on the floor, coiled around his ankles.

"I know you were an outcast," he said. "That doesn't typically leave most in your position with many options when it comes to lovers. Some men might take advantage or use your status to cause you harm."

Damn him. He sounded too genuine.

"He was a man I met and slept with of my own accord, thank you very much."

That tidbit of information didn't seem to placate him, either.

"Tell me how it happened," he insisted.

Head thrown back, she met his gaze directly and fought to suppress any ounce of shame. "I met him at the summer solstice gathering held on the grounds of a nearby coven. It is the one night of the year when witches are allowed to freely partake of wine and mingle with warlocks—"

"I know about the festivals of you pious witches," Atiernan snapped.

Apparently, his interest in this story didn't extend to learning about witch culture.

"We wear masks and dance around a bonfire," she said tersely. It felt so strange to be kneeling before him, her hands pressed against the floor rather than on his body. "It is a time when we are encouraged to indulge in our primal instincts and lower all inhibitions."

In a culture that restricted marriage to only the highest-ranking officials, the practice was one way to ensure a steady stream of new witches were born every year.

"And you chose this man?"

"He chose me," she said. Or at least, in the dreamy haze of drinking and dancing, she'd believed so.

"Did he know who you were?"

She shook her head, struck by an unexpected pain. "I snuck into the festivities. Usually, I would stay home or only watch. That year I decided to steal a mask and join in."

And she had experienced a rare, brief moment of fun that made the consequences that followed almost worth it.

"How old were you?"

"Twenty," she said. An age that felt like a lifetime ago, not less than a decade. "It was the tradition that couples could break off from the main group and bed down in the fields. So, I did."

She barely remembered the resulting act. Just that it hurt slightly and felt more like an anti-climactic tousle of sweaty bodies. Nothing momentous.

"Was he your lover for longer than a night? You didn't fear pregnancy."

"No. Is that what you want to hear? The next day, he must have realized who I was, and I never heard from him again. As for pregnancy, I am a hybrid, and I'm sure you, of all men, know we are likely infertile."

And she never dared to participate in any of the summer festivities since. She told herself heartbreak wasn't the reason. Merely disinterest. Sex hadn't been worth the risk in the long run.

"He never touched you with his fingers to make you ready for him," Atiernan surmised.

"What?" She frowned. "I don't—"

"He used you as a willing hole, but he never pleasured you. The bastard didn't even familiarize you with his cock. Did he?"

"Well, he wasn't a daemon," she spat. "One mark in his favor that you can never achieve."

"It's because I am a daemon that I know exactly what you lack," Atiernan replied. "I know how to pleasure a woman be they daemon, mortal, or witch. I know that a man should never take from a woman what he is unwilling to give, and I know this…"

He extended his hand with the palm upright. Belatedly, she realized what he wanted and left with no choice, she placed hers on top of his.

"A daemon can still please a witch, and even a witch can satisfy a daemon."

He brought her fingers to his shaft, forcing her fingers around the firm shape.

A gasp escaped her lips, echoing his own sharp intake of air. She couldn't help the sound. He felt like silk. Like molten, pulsating, steel draped in silk, shrouded by a mass of hair every bit as red as the strands growing from his scalp.

"Don't be afraid of me, witch," he goaded, sensing her apprehension. "Grip me like you handle those herbs you play with."

She tightened her grip almost spitefully, not that he seemed to mind. His spine stiffened, his eyes gleaming.

"Harder." Still manipulating her hand, he slid her coiled fingers up, nearly to the tip, then down toward the base. With every stroke, he made her go faster and tighten her grip only to release it. Then squeeze again.

Something strange happened to her body with every motion. Her skin felt tighter. Her breaths came faster. The space between her legs heated.

And he grew against her hand, lengthening, thickening.

"Take me into your mouth, witch," Atiernan commanded, presumably when he couldn't tolerate just her touch any longer.

A bubble of fear rose up, but she choked it down. Then, she leaned in, spreading her lips.

He groaned before she even made contact—first with her quivering tongue. Then her entire mouth. Even as she wrapped her lips around the rigid flesh, she was alarmed to find that she barely covered the tip.

Not that the daemon seemed to mind. The muscles of his abdomen twitched, sending a shiver through his washboard abs.

"Harder," he rasped, seeking out her gaze, his eyelids lowering. "Suck—"

She did, and an animal came to life before her. Thick fingers sank through her hair, grasping handfuls of strands.

Unguided, her fingers faltered against him before he bucked into her grip.

"Don't stop now, witch."

Impulsively, she formed a fist with him trapped in the middle, and he groaned out the most beautiful sound. Her mind reeled at the characterization, but pride no longer mattered.

The taste of him was richer than it had any right to be. Nothing foul in the slightest. Sharp and powerful and tinged with musk. She couldn't resist the urge to swallow just once, and explore what more the daemon had to offer.

At the resulting motion, a ripple ran through him, and she gasped in shock.

"Damn you." His head reared back, his eyes slits. "More."

She lowered her head and put everything from her mind but this base, primal act. Pleasing him. Making him rock into her grip. Shudder. Curse. Groan. Hiss.

Tear at her hair as if he wanted to rip out every strand in anger of what she was doing to him.

Then suddenly, he relinquished his grip.

"I suggest you release me, witch," he grated, sounding as close to breathless as someone like him could ever be. "I don't think you want my seed in your mouth."

Because he thought she'd think the act beneath her. That she'd shirk from seeing this through to its completion. That she would balk at all of him.

She didn't stop. She gripped him harder and lunged to take as much of him into her mouth as she could.

He shouted, something indecipherable.

And then she tasted hell. Wave after wave with a powerful surge that nearly knocked her back.

His seed didn't just fill her mouth, it flooded over her tongue. She stiffened, waiting to spit. Cringe. Then confusion relaxed her muscles, and she swallowed instead.

He didn't taste like a vile, disgusting substance.

He tasted like Atiernan the daemon lord—a flavor unique to him and him alone.

There was no shame in accepting it the same way she accepted his blood.

And a part of her craved to take more. All that this man could offer.

"Enough." He eased her off him and stood back. Hands braced against the wall, he panted to catch his breath while she watched.

Would he take this any further? Demand she pleasure him in other ways?

No. Without a word, he crouched to draw up his trousers and fasten them.

Then he left.

A night of hell spent tossing and turning on the sheets gave way to a dreary, rainy morning. Once the first signs of daylight ghosted the windowpanes, she crawled into the bathroom and attempted to face the mirror.

The woman she found staring back looked nothing like the Miranda Lightwood she'd come to expect. This woman looked...ravaged, her lips swollen and glistening. Head bowed, she rinsed out her mouth and raked her fingers through her tangled hair.

Cleaned and dressed, she couldn't escape to Peony's store-room fast enough.

The woman greeted her at the doorway, her lips pursed in an unusually serious expression. "I want to apologize for what happened," she said, pushing her filthy glasses further up the bridge of her nose. "In all reality, I meant merely to spike your tea daily with a long-acting poison and give you the antidote once Atiernan decided to return you to your coven. It was a failsafe, really."

"I know," Miranda admitted. Would she have done any differently were the roles reversed? Probably not.

"Good," Peony said, shuffling inside her workshop. "Then you can consider us even, given that you had Atiernan strongarm me into this situation."

"What?" Confused, Miranda followed the woman inside and instantly saw what she meant. In addition to the bespectacled mage, a beaming Beth stood in the center of the room, her hair in pigtails and a white apron slung over the front of her gray pinafore.

"Atiernan said I can help today," she chirped, making it clear that her mother was not of the same mind. "I'm guessing you talked to him. Whatever you told him worked! Thank you!"

Miranda swayed, feeling her cheeks catch fire.

Peony didn't seem angry, however. She merely nodded toward a pile of assembled herbs and rolled up her sleeves.

"There have been sightings of sentinels in the area, and there is much to be done. We need to prepare in case of another breach. This isn't a game, Bethaem," the mage added with a disapproving glance in the girl's direction. "You will be expected to work."

Moments later, they were neck-deep in said work, with each woman occupied with various sets of tasks.

"Like this?" Beth asked while arranging a roll of bandages beside where Miranda stirred a steaming pot of brew.

"Yes," Miranda said with a nod. "You learn fast."

"But you still have miles to go," Peony warned from across the room. While stern, no one could mishear the note of grudging approval in her tone. "Now, less chatter and more work."

And more still.

They had to replenish Peony's stocks of salve in case there were any wounded. There were new charms to craft and potions to stockpile.

And other, more personal, potions Miranda itched to devise with Atiernan in mind. She hadn't lied when she told him she might be infertile—*might* being the key word. So much of what her mother and her acolytes told her had already turned out to be a lie. Why take the risk?

Because, she knew as surely as the sun rising and setting every day, that Atiernan would have her soon. Any way he wanted, and she wouldn't be able to stop him.

Not because of force, either…

Which was the terrifying part.

Her lips ached with the knowledge of what she'd already done of her own free will. On the one hand, the memories horrified her. On the other…

Years of crafting and honing spells, and she had never felt more powerful than in that moment. The realization unnerved her. Terrified. With only her body at her disposal, she'd brought a man like Atiernan to his knees. She'd held him—literally—in the palm of her hand, and she knew his pleasure hadn't been faked.

Nothing in either the arsenal of witch magic or even blood magic had filled her with the same terrible feeling of absolute power over something that could bend and break her. Or empower her beyond reason.

"Are we supposed to let it burn like that?"

Miranda startled to awareness as Beth wrinkled her nostrils at the substance bubbling away in the cauldron before her. No, such a potion was not meant to be burned. Just like that, hours of work had been ruined.

She kept the failure to herself as she lifted the pot and carried it to the bucket Peony had designated for waste. With fresh ingredients and a clean vessel, she began again, paying close attention to every measurement and portion of liquid.

"Is magic always like this?" Beth asked, still by her side. "So… Boring?"

Miranda laughed. "Perhaps," she conceded. "Though I never found it dull."

There was a time when she hadn't been able to practice honest magic at all. Only in secret with whatever knowledge she'd gleaned through stray texts or overheard. Via such rudimentary methods, she'd burned herself more often than not and created enough failed potions to dismay any fledgling witch.

Still, she persisted for one reason and one reason alone.

"It's in my blood," she admitted. "I don't think I could ever do anything but use nature as it was always intended. To help and to heal."

Perhaps, one day, she might right the wrong her birth wrought upon the world. A woman could hope.

"Magic is a study," Peony pitched in from across the room. "Like any craft, it must be carefully learned and respected. You won't find pixie dust and dramatic explosions here. Perhaps you might find yourself better entertained outside, Bethaem? There you can run and play with the other children—"

"I'm fine," Beth said, stubbornly squaring her chin. "I want to learn. I won't complain."

"Good." Peony sighed. "Then let us work. There is much to be done. Like caring for your friend in the dungeon, for instance?"

Miranda balked. She'd nearly forgotten of the creature Atiernan had procured for her.

"We can't hold such a beast for very long," Peony added. "I had the kitchens feed it whatever scraps they could part with, but that will not satisfy the monster. We must dispose of it soon."

Miranda nodded. "This will come in handy—" she nodded to the fresh iteration of her potion, now simmering a beautiful silver color rather than a blackened brown. "It should be ready in a few more hours. But…"

She hesitated before voicing yet another task waiting to be accomplished.

"I will need to consult Marcus. This was his plan, after all. He might have another idea in mind, should mine fail."

Instantly, all traces of goodwill left Peony's expression, rendering her as hard as a statue. "That you can do alone. Bethaem, tend Miranda's potion—and pay attention. Let it burn again, and I will tan your hide. As for the…guest," the mage added, obviously tailoring her word choice. "You can find him in the great hall under guard. They should not stop you from speaking to him. I just ask that you be careful. The most base of daemons pray on our weaknesses. Such as lust, fear, or loneliness. You must not let them do so."

Apparently, Peony thought her so weak that she'd fall for any attempt on Marcus' behalf to trick her, merely because they shared similar origins. *No.* She shook her head to banish the paranoia. The truth could have been far simpler —Peony was afraid and had every right to be on guard where the safety of her family was concerned.

"I'll be careful," Miranda replied, relinquishing her spot to Beth. "I promise."

"Good." Peony's voice chased her into the hall. "I will hold you to that."

EIGHT

As far as prison arrangements went, Marcus' were admittedly a step up from what hers had been initially. Rather than the dungeons, Atiernan's men had sequestered him in a corner of the great hall free from any windows or furniture, apart from a thin mattress and a bucket. Despite his fairly-comfortable quarters, Marcus didn't seem content in the least.

He paced, his arms crossed, head held in a way eerily similar to Atiernan whenever he plotted some devious way to torment her next.

The comparison made Miranda swallow, and her steps faltered just beyond the threshold of the chamber.

"You should not be here," the posted guard snarled, eyeing her with abject disgust. "Two abominations conspiring together? Not on my watch."

So much for Peony's insistence that she wouldn't be hassled.

Miranda cocked her head, prepared to issue a scathing reply.

"I suggest you tailor your speech," Marcus called from the center of his chamber before she could utter a word. He stood still, his eyes cloaked in the shadow cast by his long, unruly hair. "Unless you want your lord to take his ire out on you."

"Silence!" the guard snapped. "Keep your meddling words to yourself, half-breed."

"Half-breed or not, I have eyes," Marcus replied, but rather than anger, his tone concealed a hint of laughter. "See those marks on her neck? I can assure you that one of your comrades or any other man for that matter didn't put them there. Your lord did. You're speaking to *his* woman, and if he sent her here to do his bidding, I suggest you let her pass."

Miranda felt her cheeks flame, though she couldn't deny the effect the words had. The guard paled, his expression wary.

"Good boy," Marcus quipped. "Come in, Miranda. It's about time you paid me a visit."

She didn't miss the quiet jab concealed within the greeting. What might have been guilt coiled in her stomach. After all, she'd torn this man from his own realm and left him to rot while dallying with the daemon lord holding him prisoner.

Head lowered, she entered the room, coming as close to him as she dared. When she opened her mouth, demands for his assistance weren't the first words to spring from her lips.

"I'm… Sorry," she rasped. "I brought you here. You had no say. I apologize for the way you've been treated."

Marcus shrugged, but she couldn't tell what he truly thought. His eyes were unreadable, more guarded than even Atiernan's. Though, he had no idea that it was one of the few times she'd ever willingly apologized to anyone.

The words seemed to stick in her throat for that reason, weighed down by guilt. She meant what she'd said. She truly was sorry.

"I take it that Atiernan hasn't sent you here as a gesture of good will?" he dryly remarked.

"No," she admitted. "I came on my own. I wanted to talk to you about… Your mother."

She knew the damage those two words could inspire on her alone. Atiernan openly praised his upbringing, and Beth seemed to adore Peony, despite her strict parenting. Still, Miranda couldn't deny some grim, fragile comradery at the way Marcus flinched at the mere mention of the woman who bore him.

"Liva the witch," he said with all the enthusiasm of someone discussing a topic they despised. "What do you want to know? Though, I'm sure Atiernan can tell you far more about her than I can."

He could—though at a price she was still hesitant to pay. Honestly, if she truly inspected her reasons for questioning him, Liva's power and legacy were low on the list. Her motives were entirely selfish. Childish.

"I want to know what it was like," she said softly. "Growing up with her as a mother."

Marcus raised an eyebrow. "You mean was it all blood rites, orgies, and sacrifices? Not quite."

His smile invited her closer, and the feeling seemed to be mutual. When he positioned himself against a far wall and sat down, she copied him while keeping a fair bit of space between them.

"When were you born?" Miranda asked when he fell silent. "You must be as long-lived as Atiernan, surely."

An age the former had hinted spanned thousands of years.

Marcus chuckled, his upper lip quirked. Surprisingly, the expression revealed the absence of fangs. His teeth were as normally shaped as hers were.

"We went over this, remember? If you consider twenty-eight ancient, then yes. I am very long-lived."

An answering laugh trickled from her throat before she could help it. "I thought you might have been playing coy," she admitted. "I just can't believe we're the same age."

She marveled at that. He and Atiernan physically looked as though a handful of years separated them. Not millennia. But his proposed age posed another question.

"How? Atiernan claims he hasn't seen Liva in centuries."

There was the possibility the daemon could have lied to her, and that his claims about his celibacy were as flimsy as her insistence on being a full-blooded witch.

"I'm not entirely sure," Marcus admitted, his chin tilted thoughtfully. "It's a question I've spent most of my life trying to answer. A few years ago, however, I met a witch who gave me an idea of how it might have been done. I was conceived the natural way during their relationship, but before I came to term, my mother used magic to conceal me somewhere. The only problem with that theory is the vessel would need to be a living being. Once placed there, I wouldn't be able to be moved."

"But if it was destroyed?" Miranda asked. It was a chilling theory that nonetheless thrilled the part of her brain that loved applying magical knowledge to the universe's many mysteries.

"I would either die or be born naturally, depending on the nature of what contained me. However, the hole in that theory is that, no mortal and few immortals could live centuries. Liva didn't carry me to term herself for a reason, though I have yet to discover that, either."

He frowned, consumed by the logical conundrum in a way that even Atiernan had yet to display. The sight reminded her of how greedily she used to spy on the other witches and incorporate the smallest hint of knowledge into a spell or potion.

Rarely did she have someone to bounce ideas off. Or a friend to talk to.

"It makes sense, your theory," she admitted, leaning back against the wall. "But you're right—there are limitations. The vessel would need to be living for all those years, and protected from any outside forces. Not to mention, your mother must have had a way of retrieving you when you were born."

"It's not like I can ask her," he said with a harsh laugh.

"She didn't raise you?"

He continued to chuckle as if her question were a harmless joke. "No. Liva is my mother only in the most basic definition of the word. I've only met her a handful of times since my birth, all brief, none of them pleasant."

He said it so casually, but Miranda felt her eyes bulge.

"She didn't keep you? But then why…"

He shifted to face her, and curiosity glinted openly in his dark eyes. "Why what?"

She hesitated. Was playing show and tell with a stranger a helpful pastime with all that loomed over her head? No. Still, something in her couldn't resist the freedom to speak openly about what she'd spent her entire life carrying in secret.

"Why did she have you?" she asked. No longer could she look at Marcus, though. Instead, she eyed a corner of the room and tried to keep her expression blank. No tears. Gods, no more tears. "Why bring you to term if not to use you for your blood?"

She'd already seen his arms and the lack of scars on them. Neither did he seem familiar or comfortable with using his blood outside of the most rudimentary of spells.

"Why did she have you if not to use you for her own means?"

Her voice echoed brokenly, hoarse with the confusion of the little girl she used to be.

"I don't know," Marcus admitted. "I'm sure she plans to use us—me, in some way or another. I haven't figured out how. The few theories I have come up with? Not pretty. Though, that isn't what you meant, is it?"

Miranda shook her head, too overwhelmed to speak.

Apparently, she didn't need to. Marcus cocked his head and fixed her with a searching look. Voice soft, he said, "Your mother used you to practice blood magic."

It sounded so dirty when said out loud. Vile. Agatha Lightwood would scoff at the insinuation, but it was the truth. The grim, horrible truth.

"Yes," Miranda rasped. "That's all I ever was to her. A tool to use to achieve her own aims."

"I'm sorry." He meant it, too, another realization that floored her. First daemons, now another half-breed. All of whom showed her far more respect than anyone in her coven ever had.

And yet, you still plan to grovel for the witches' acceptance, a part of her snarled.

"Liva never taught me magic," Marcus admitted. "I wish she had. I could use that magic against her or find out what she's planning."

"No," Miranda said softly. "You don't. That kind of magic is… It isn't natural. To channel it is excruciating—"

"Even when you used it to bring me here? We can pretend like I crafted the spell, but you and I know the truth. It was your blood and your skill that brought us here. You merely carried me along for the ride."

She nodded, feeling a tear slip down her cheek before she could stop it. "It hurts every time. It's like I'm being burned alive from the inside out. An agony I wouldn't wish even on my worst enemy."

"I'll take your word for it," Marcus said. "But I spent most of my life powerless. I think I would have given anything to have a small semblance of my power with which to fight back."

But she hadn't fought back. Not once. Every day of the past twenty-eight years, she'd submitted herself to the crone's bidding, doing whatever she asked. There had never been a choice.

"I think I would have preferred to be like you," she said softly. "To make my own way and not be confined by what I am."

"We are confined," Marcus said. Without warning, he brought himself closer and extended a hand. It was calloused, with the palm worn and rugged.

Warily, Miranda took it anyway.

"But not by what we are," Marcus continued. "By them. Those who would cast blame on us for our parents' sins. We can't help that. We were merely born into this world with no say in our nature. But I can tell you this. We feel like everyone else. We grieve like everyone else. We hurt like everyone else. We can tolerate their prejudices but never accept them. We deserve to live as they do. No matter if they want to admit it or not."

Miranda eyed their clasped fingers, sensing unexpected similarities she hadn't noticed at first glance. Like how they were the same skin tone and held onto each other with the same awkward familiarity.

As if they weren't used to being willingly touched, not by anyone. The realization humbled her in a way nothing else had. It was harrowing to realize that, after years of enduring scorn and derision, she wasn't alone in that experience.

"Tell me about the woman who raised you," she said gently, genuinely curious.

"My *real* mother," Marcus replied, but his expression softened in a way that made it clear that whatever he felt toward her was nothing compared to his hatred toward Liva. "She is a witch, though not from any coven you'll know. She took me in when I was a child, already bitter with the experiences I'd lived through. Words can't describe the patience she possessed when raising me. I won't deny it —I didn't want love. Didn't want help or affection. She gave me that and more anyway."

"She didn't teach you magic, though," Miranda pointed out. Was she jealous? Maybe not. In a sense, her mother hadn't taught her magic either. She learned from watching and listening, striving to hone her skill with honest spell craft as if to make up for her usage of blood magic. That hunger for knowledge alone proved her to be a true witch in more ways than one. Never would she regret that.

"No," Marcus said. "I think she would have, if I asked her to, but I was more interested in scaling the trees around our home and trying to eat the edible berries in her garden."

Miranda felt a laugh escape her at the mental image. "I can't imagine she enjoyed that too much."

He laughed as well, and she was alarmed to find the sound every bit as rich and booming as one of Atiernan's. "No. One time she nearly tanned my hide when I strayed too close to the poisonous plants. Not because she thought I might damage them, but because she feared I'd be stupid enough to eat one. She was a good woman."

Miranda felt her heart constrict. "Was?"

"She's still alive. I just… I haven't visited her in a while. Even if Liva knows about her, I won't give the bitch any reason to use her life as a pawn."

Meaning that he'd willfully chosen to cut himself off from the only family he'd known. Miranda felt an odd sense of déjà vu unfurl in her chest.

Whether Atiernan believed him or not, Marcus seemed like the man in one way—both men valued their family above all else.

No matter the cost to themselves.

Atiernan stewed in petty irritation for most of the day. He discussed new patrol schedules with Ben and the other guards. He reviewed their food stores and renegotiated some of the prices his people paid for the goods they imported from the wider realm. In other words—he did everything he could to put off finding the witch until the very last second. Only when darkness fell did he finally leave his study in search of the woman.

But she wasn't in Peony's storeroom.

"I haven't seen her for hours," the mage admitted, an eyebrow raised in alarm. It was no small feat that Atiernan could see her at all, considering the room was filled with varying shades of green and yellow smoke.

Even Beth seemed fittingly engrossed in whatever concoctions they were currently brewing. From her position hunched on the floor, she barely tossed Atiernan a wave by way of greeting.

It annoyed him to admit that Miranda might have had the right idea to recommend the girl study magic. At least she could interact with her mother without being scolded at every turn for once.

But, while the witch might have done one good deed, who knew what other schemes she had in mind. Gone for hours. That wasn't a promising sign.

"That doesn't seem like you, Peony," Atiernan said, grappling for control. "To let our captive witch out of your sight to do gods know what damage in the meantime."

His tone served to draw a wince from the mage, at least. She stood back from her cauldron and faced him, hands on her bony hips.

"I know where she *went*," the woman conceded, and Atiernan's unease instantly grew. She'd obscured that fact for a reason. Her wary glance in his direction proved it. "She must still be there."

"Where?"

"With the half-breed. Oh, don't look at me like that," the mage huffed. "She claimed interest in speaking to him alone. I merely told her where he was."

"So, they can conspire together," Atiernan growled, curling his hands into fists. It was a tone he rarely used on Peony, if ever.

The mage had the sense to sigh and cock her head in a semblance of guilt. "She can be convincing when she wants to be—"

"Don't play coy. You relent to no one."

Peony shrugged. "And…"

"And what?" Atiernan bellowed, though mentally, he was already running through the various ways he'd punish the witch. After he wrought out whatever secrets she divulged to the imposter. And he would be very creative in devising how.

"And, she looked like a little girl desperate to feel, even for a second, like she wasn't alone. How could I deny her that?"

Damn her. He hated when she weaponized her maternal instincts. Usually, it was to his benefit, or Bethaem's. Rarely someone else's, and certainly not a witch.

"She wants to learn from him, I think," Beth pitched in, still hunched over a cauldron. "I would if I were in her shoes."

"What do you mean?"

The girl looked up, her eyes partially obscured by her messy, disheveled bangs. "He's someone like her. She's probably curious about him. I would be."

Like her. Atiernan doubted that characterization. Miranda was many things, but—as he was grudgingly starting to understand—she was not evil. Not entirely. She experienced emotion on a level that seemed far beyond anything a creature like Liva could.

And any being born from that bitch would be one and the same. A monster—whether it claimed to share his blood or not.

"I will find her," he growled, heading for the door.

"Atiernan," Peony called after him. "You will not scold her like some wayward little girl."

A rich ask, considering the comparison she herself had made just seconds prior.

"You will *listen* to her," the woman went on, her voice chasing him into the hall. "Listen and discern from her whether or not we can trust her judgment."

Instantly, he sensed what Peony truly meant—she was worried. For whatever reason, she didn't know what to make of the man who called himself his son.

But Atiernan was willing to pass judgment for them both.

Marcus couldn't be trusted.

"I'll find her," he reiterated.

And whatever punishment he bestowed upon the witch would be his alone to decide. In this one arena, Peony held no sway.

He alone would serve as judge, jury, and executioner.

And he would pass judgment on Miranda Lightwood however he damn well saw fit.

He neared the room they kept the prisoner in, unsure of what to expect. Them, heads bowed together, plotting his destruction at Liva's behest? That would at least be preferable to the sound that greeted him instead.

Not furious muttering, but… Laughter.

Hers.

The delicate notes stopped him short. Fangs bared, he listened, aware of the guard gaping in his direction. Instantly, he could recognize that the sound differed from the forced, haughty laughs she issued around him. It was lighter. Musical. Beautiful.

And it was entirely for the imposter's benefit.

"Open the door," he growled, and the guard rushed to obey.

The suddenness startled the two within, catching them both mid-chuckle. They sat on the floor, unusually close. The witch had her hand inches near the male's knee, and Atiernan noted that she didn't cringe from his touch—their forearms brushed each other's openly. Though, that was where the intimacy ended.

Still, he felt his vision turn red around the edges, and he wasn't fully aware of the words he said next. Just that the woman flinched and lurched to her feet.

"She meant no harm." The voice came from the man beside her, but Atiernan didn't spare him a single glance. Instead, his gaze bore into her, and to his shock, she held his stare unflinchingly.

"Is something wrong?" she asked.

"Come," he snarled, storming into the hall.

He didn't turn to see that she followed—her soft steps echoed loudly enough. Still, some part of him acknowledged that fear wasn't what drove her, and neither was obedience. Just curiosity.

He'd barged in there like a jealous young buck, and the witch couldn't resist probing his reaction. It was another way she diverged from Liva's cold, calculating approach to conversation. The latter expected obsession and devotion from any fool to cross her orbit.

Miranda, however, seemed stunned that he even cared that she met with his enemy behind closed doors.

"You cannot ignore him forever, you do realize," she said. Her voice had regained its typical hostile cadence. Good. Now that he knew her range could extend beyond pleasured moans and cold conversation, he better understood how far the woman could be pushed.

Though her laughter shouldn't have confounded him so damn much. Nor the smile he glimpsed before she noticed his presence.

"I think you should speak to him," she went on, following him up the main staircase. "How else will you know for sure if you can trust him—"

"It is you who should be concerned about my trust." He reached back for her wrist and pulled her along. His pace was ruthless, and he knew she struggled to keep up as he marched down the upstairs hallway and entered the room beside his.

Her eyes widened in recognition—was she surprised he hadn't brought her to the dungeons? Though with her pet still below, there wasn't exactly room.

Spinning to face her, Atiernan coincidentally put himself between her and the only exit.

"What did he say to you?"

The witch frowned, her eyes wary. "He told me about his mother. His upbringing—"

"No." He advanced, herding her into a corner. "What did he say to make you laugh?"

Her brows furrowed as if she didn't understand what he meant. "I... I don't remember... Oh—" A sudden gasp revealed that she did remember after all.

"Will you enlighten me now?"

"He told me about the woman who raised him," she said, her expression awed. "How she used to chase him around her garden when he tried to eat her herbs. How she would feed him medicinal soup when he was sick. The way she cared for him."

Atiernan felt his eyes narrow. "That doesn't sound like Liva."

"No." Miranda shook her head. "She wasn't Liva."

Then who raised the creature? He shied away from the thought. No one good. A woman like Peony wouldn't have been fooled by such a beast.

A daemon-witch hybrid could only mean trouble.

Though, he seemed to have no problem with the woman standing before him now. A part of him tried to rationalize it with the simple observation that Miranda was different. She wasn't evil, though her mother had certainly used her for such purposes. He remembered what Beth had said. Perhaps the young fledgling had more insight than he gave her credit for?

"You feel sympathy with him. With it."

"Of course, I do." Her chin jutted into the air as she took offense to the mere suggestion that she shouldn't. "He is a person. He has treated me kindly. If I can tolerate you, I can certainly stomach another hybrid."

"And just how did you tolerate him?" Damn. He hated the raw grit in his voice. It alone revealed far more anger than he was willing to admit. Jealousy, too.

Luckily for him, Miranda seemed too innocent—or oblivious to her own appeal—and the insinuation seemed to go right over her head.

"I at least can talk to him," she countered, chin in the air. "Maybe you should try it? He may be every bit as evil as you think he is. You will never know unless you speak to him directly."

"Or perhaps you can do all the talking for us both?" he tossed back. A glance at her revealed that her cheeks were reddened. Finally, she'd sensed what he'd been implying all along.

"You think I'm attracted to him."

"Are you?" A growl crept into his voice as his muscles tensed in anticipation of her answer.

Should she say yes…

He'd kill the imposter with his bare hands. Rip him to pieces, then dare her to laugh around him the way she had around it.

"I am busy, daemon," she replied. "I want to go home. To do that, I need to fulfill our bargain. To do that, I need Marcus."

Marcus. Again, she referred to him by name. Though why shouldn't she? Hissing, Atiernan raked a hand through his hair and tried to focus. Jealousy was such a pesky fucking emotion. He hadn't experienced it in…

Far too long.

"Need him how?" he asked offhandedly.

"Capturing the creature was his idea," Miranda pointed out. "Together, we can devise a weapon to defeat them."

"And plot on how to destroy me in the meantime?"

"No. What? Do you need me to make yet another bargain?" she asked. "If Marcus betrays you, you can kill us both—"

"No." He grabbed her wrist, yanking her closer. Her fragile body collided with his chest, so damn warm. "If Marcus betrays me, you alone will atone for every last sin. You will never see your coven again, witch. You will stay here, with me, for all eternity."

When said out loud, it didn't sound like such a horrid fate to his ears. His brain skipped ahead, conjuring plenty of tasks he could assign to the witch, designed to keep her busy for decades. Fed on a steady supply of his blood, she would live for far longer than she otherwise would.

And he aimed to take advantage of every tortured second of her existence.

But to her, those words resonated as if he'd damned her to Hell.

"You think I would harm you." He captured her cheek against his palm, feeling her shiver in response.

"You will," she whispered, recoiling from his touch.

But would he? Gazing into her eyes, he couldn't envision purposefully doing anything to cause her pain. And that terrified the hell out of him.

"Fine." He stood back, though he kept his mouth near enough to her ear so that she could miss none of what he said. "I will let you work with Marcus... In exchange for one thing."

"What?"

Internally, he chuckled at how she couldn't resist making a bargain. Her father may have been a twisted, daemonic soul, but she had inherited the defining trait of a Vaer daemon, alright.

"An orgasm," he said in response to her questioning expression.

Without one shred of guilt, he relished how she reacted to that proposal. Her eyes widened, and her cheeks flamed. No one would guess that just hours ago, those pert little lips had been wrapped around his cock. And brought him a pleasure he couldn't remember ever experiencing before.

If he'd wanted her to balk at the request, her prideful glare demolished that hope. "If debasing myself is what it takes to find the answers to your problems, then so be it, daemon—"

"I never said the orgasm would be experienced by me," he countered. Before she could react, he caught her waist and brought her to the bed. There, he let her fall.

A gasp escaped her as she landed on the mattress upright, her chest heaving.

"It will be yours, experienced to prove that pain isn't all I can give to you."

Something he suddenly felt determined to make clear. An eternity with him wouldn't mean torture for the witch necessarily. Just for him. Years of knowing he could never make her laugh the way another man did so easily. Years of questioning if her orgasms for him until now had been real or faked. Years of trying to unravel the mystery of this infuriating woman.

"W-Wait," she gasped as he crouched at the edge of the bed before her trembling legs. "I want something too."

Of course, she did—a Vaer through and through.

"Strange for a prisoner to make a request," he countered gruffly. The argument became moot the second he palmed a slender thigh—she could have asked for the world, and he would have given it to her. Anything to make her legs part of their own accord, though she held her breath in anticipation. "What?"

"I want the truth," she said. "If Marcus is your son… Why not speak to him?"

He frowned. Puzzled by the reaction, he nuzzled a delicate knee and sensed the pulse swishing beneath her skin.

"Tell me," she croaked. "And you can have…"

She couldn't even put it into words. The promise alone was enough to move him, however.

He hissed out an answer through clenched teeth. "Because to acknowledge him as my son would mean…" Frustrated, he bared his fangs but didn't bite. Instead, he teased a strip of thin flesh, lapping at the stinging pricks with his tongue.

She inhaled raggedly at the sensation, and the gap between her thighs widened, enough for him to fit his head between them. Her heat ghosted his face, and he felt his cock harden in response. Strange. He'd already experienced her in every way but with his cock. One might think that would be enough to temper the lust.

Instead, her nearness just hit him harder. Stronger. With every passing second, his need for her only grew, festering into a painful craving. An addiction. One he feared no amount of sex could ever satisfy.

"Tell me," she whimpered as his mouth inched higher along her thigh. He still had yet to bite—each brush of his lips could be construed as a featherlight kiss instead. "Why?"

"Because it would mean I failed him," he grated through clenched teeth. "I failed the one task any father should fulfill first and foremost. I left him to the whims of that evil bitch. How could I face him after that?"

And how could the resulting man ever forgive him, let alone grow up untainted by Liva's cruelty? In the long run, it would be better to turn his back on such a creature or otherwise risk…

A pain like no other. Centuries later, Peony still mourned her son to the extent that she could hardly bear to say his name. He knew it hurt her just to breathe without him. To know in her soul that he was gone, and she would never ever be able to fill the void left behind.

How could he mourn for a son he never even knew existed?

"You are afraid," Miranda gasped, as if the prospect confused her. Thrilled her. The witch had found a weakness of his to exploit.

Would she rush to do so?

"I am cautious," he warned. "As you should be. Nothing good ever came from Liva—"

"I came from her," the witch countered. Before he could reach another conclusion, she added, "From the land she founded. The coven she created. I may not have sprung from her womb, but in a way, I came from her as much as Marcus did. Am I evil?"

No. Or, if she were capable of such vile evil, he had yet to see any trace of it. A witch who strived to honor the very coven that ostracized her. The woman who didn't resent the mother who tormented her. A haughty captive who didn't hesitate to save a daemon teenager even at the risk of her own life.

Miranda wasn't evil, but her true nature eluded him, even now.

Rather than ponder such a conundrum, he pushed the skirt of her dress up to her waist and scrutinized the flesh bared to him. A groan caught in his chest. All thoughts of his enemies forgotten, he raked his gaze from the creamy skin of her thighs up to the thatch of dark curls awaiting between them.

"I think you are many things, witch," he told her, lowering his head. "But I will take my payment now. Do as you wish, but do not expect me to play Liva's game."

He was already trapped within the web of another cunning witch.

Though he wasn't sure just yet if he was inclined to escape it.

Not without a fight.

Miranda despaired. There was no way she could fight the daemon off—but that wasn't what made her pulse race and belly tighten in defeat. No. It was the simple fact that she didn't *want* to.

Her eyes were riveted to the scarlet hair draping Atiernan like a fiery cape. She didn't dare look away for even a second. Not until she finally felt…

Hellfire.

His tongue stabbed like a lance, aiming directly for her sex. Gods help her—she didn't evade the contact like she should have. Instead, her traitorous hips arched, seeming to welcome the invading pressure.

Welcome *him*.

A low sound rumbled from his direction, resonating through her in a dangerous shiver. Her eyelids fluttered as the heat from his mouth invaded her body with every rough stroke.

There wasn't any thought in her mind to resist. Just endure.

He felt so…good. Her own fingers couldn't bring the kind of pleasure he did merely with his mouth. Then, without warning, he latched onto her aching flesh completely and sucked.

Her cry echoed off the walls, shrill and foreign.

Easily overpowering it was Atiernan's growl. A sign of anger? No. Horror dawned over her as he reared back, meeting her gaze with a shocked expression.

"A witch in pleasure at the mercy of a daemon?" His fangs flashed, transforming his grin into something feral. "Say it isn't so."

"No!" She attempted to draw her knees together, bargain be damned. Nothing was worth her pride. Right?

Wrong. One caress of a calloused hand along her inner thigh and her legs sprung apart. Eagerly, he sank between them and found her again. He added a finger. Then another. More, assaulting her tender flesh with an intensity that had her rocking back and forth.

"Damn," the daemon rasped. "I've had more women than you can imagine. None have ever felt like you."

Her cheeks flamed. Lies, of course. He was feeding her the same lines he told all his many women. How beautiful they were. How perfect.

"I've felt your arousal before," Atiernan went on. "But I have yet to hear you moan as if your coven isn't listening."

The implication made her flinch. Then his thumb invaded her, and her world narrowed to the sensation of his thick finger easing inside her channel.

Another gasp broke loose, and he chuckled in triumph.

"I want to hear that sound, very much, Miranda. Give it to me—"

"I'll give..." Her heart lurched. Was that really her voice? Had she gone insane? "But only if... Only if you let him in."

Marcus. He should have been the furthest thing from her mind at the moment—and maybe he was. His face wasn't the one lurking in her head as she pondered the reasons behind her request.

She knew what it was like to be shunned by a parent, but she couldn't fathom the pain of not knowing her own child. She liked to think she would have raised hers differently, half-daemon or not.

"Please..."

Atiernan didn't respond. Instead, he refocused his efforts. No longer was he merely tasting with his tongue. He lunged as if aiming to devour her.

A string of noises left her throat, each more broken than the last. They echoed ceaselessly as her hips rocked against the assaulting force.

Gods only knew how she managed to keep a coherent thought in her head, let alone one that wasn't fixated on the coven or the light wood tree.

Just him.

"Promise me—" Her words ended on a whine as he used two fingers to stretch her open for his tongue to slither in between.

"Give me what I seek, witch," he spoke against her sensitive flesh, "and I will give you whatever the hell you desire."

There wasn't time to doubt him. At his words, she broke.

For a dangerous few seconds, she didn't care what she did or what noises she made. She merely endured the pleasure washing over her in long, glorious waves drawn out by his constantly lapping tongue.

The daemon drank from her as if crazed. Every drop of arousal he rushed to steal with increasing ferocity.

She didn't know how long it lasted. Just that when she finally regained her senses, writhing on the twisted sheets, the daemon was hunched over her.

He said nothing as he stood, his lips glistening. Then he cocked his head.

"Tomorrow, you can play your games with Marcus. Tonight, you lie there and think of nothing but me."

Before she'd finished catching her breath, he was gone.

THE NEXT MORNING, Miranda couldn't escape her room fast enough. She paused only to bathe and get dressed in a simple brown dress borrowed from Peony. Then she darted into the corridor and raced to the great hall before anyone else could consider joining her. For a moment, she feared someone had found her after all—soft footsteps echoed in her wake—but when she glanced over her shoulder, no one was in view.

Thank the gods.

She wasn't afraid. Still, she breathed a sigh of relief when she found no one beside Marcus' door but the guard.

Atiernan must have told him what to expect, because he stood aside and beckoned Marcus out. Then he acted as their silent guard as they headed to the dungeons.

"So, what exactly is your plan?" she asked Marcus.

He inclined his head, his expression thoughtful. "These creatures bleed, yes?"

She nodded, picturing the blackish substance she'd seen drip from the sentinel's hulking bodies.

"Well, perhaps with your magic and my skill, we can devise a way to use it to our benefit."

She raised an eyebrow. "Like by deriving a poison from it?"

Marcus chuckled. "Exactly. Though one that can apply to the entire race."

He trailed off as they reached the dungeon and a ferocious growl resonated through the spacious chamber. The sound ripped through Miranda, rousing a fear she didn't appreciate the full extent of until now. Her neck ached as if remembering the agony of the creature's bite.

"It looks like our quarry is adjusting well to the accommodations," Marcus said dryly.

A massive sentinel lurked in a cell only slightly larger than the one Atiernan had kept her in. Black blood covered its torso, where Miranda suspected a chunk of its flesh was missing. As they neared, the beast rammed itself against the metal bars, creating a deafening clamor.

"You should finish your work quickly so we can kill it, witch," the guard remarked coldly. "Nothing good comes from keeping such a beast here. Such unnatural abominations cannot be trusted."

"Point taken," Marcus said, raising his voice. "We can handle things from here. You can wait near the steps."

The man scoffed. "As if I would ever leave the two of you. You'll free the beast and set it loose."

"Then wouldn't it be better for you to be by the door, prepared to face such a threat and raise the alarm, than right here to serve as fitting food for our hungry friend?" Marcus pointed out.

With a wary glance in their direction, the man retreated.

"That was a clever trick," Miranda remarked.

"Clever or foolish to put a man who despises us by our only exit," Marcus said with a shrug. "Still, I never worked well in a hostile environment."

"Is that why you live in the mortal realm?" She didn't know why the prospect intrigued her so much. A bar in a small town off a busy highway seemed like such an unlikely place for the son of a daemon lord.

And yet, here she was—a captive woman masquerading as a pure-blood witch. In reality, her father was a monster as long-lived as Atiernan, yet her life wasn't anything special.

Perhaps that was what befitted such terrifying, unholy men. Hybrid children cursed to bear the weight of their many sins in obscurity.

"I live in the mortal realm because I grew up there," Marcus replied. He began to pace the length of the creature's cell, inspecting every inch of the beast within. "I can't deny that I prefer the mortal one after what little time I've spent here. Humans are just as likely to put a knife in my back, but at least they won't use my blood in a ritual to devise dark magic while they're at it."

"But your knife isn't from the mortal realm."

She'd caught only a glimpse of the blade—usually kept in a black, leather sheath—but she remembered that, amid the chaos of their arrival, Marcus had requested it be kept safe. Though he didn't carry it on him now, she suspected Peony had honored his request.

"It means a lot to you," she added when he said nothing.

"One could say that," he said. "That knife is the one thing Liva ever gave me. I suppose I could call it a gift. Or a curse."

"Oh?"

"Later. Mementos from my mother aren't important right now. Look at the beast—" he nodded toward the snarling creature, its fangs bared. "Look into its eyes and tell me what you see."

Remembering the monster that attacked her, Miranda hesitated. "I'm not sure what exactly I'm meant to find."

"Trust me. Just try."

With a sigh, she raised her head, peering into the creature's soulless gaze. Though, on second thought… It didn't stare at her with raw hunger like a rat might. Neither did it stare through her. Instead, those scarlet irises bore directly into hers. Almost as if…

"It's looking right at me. Like it's—"

"Intelligent," Marcus finished for her. "Not a dumb, mindless beast but one with intellect. Cunning."

"One attacked me before. But I heard it speak. It called for Atiernan—"

Suddenly the monster lunged, rattling the bars with an ominous thud.

"I believe you," Marcus said, taking a step back. "In fact, I think this monster understood you as well."

"Why does it matter?"

He gave her an odd look. "Because a creature that can understand can be reasoned with. Don't you want to know the truth behind these attacks?"

It was a viewpoint Miranda hadn't considered. Treat the beast not like a monster deserving death but as a living, thinking being with a mind of its own? Ironically, the former method was how most witches seemed to deal with her.

"Why? Even if it has intellect, as you say, why does that matter?"

Marcus met her gaze, but again, his eyes were unreadable, merely displaying her reflection. Bathed in shadow and torchlight, she resembled something as unseemly as the creature locked within the cage.

"You know why it matters," he said. "The same way it matters when someone assumes that between the two of us, all we think about is power and domination. Understand your enemy, and you can better learn how to defeat it. Or, how to coexist with it."

Much like Atiernan seemed determined to break inside her mind and utilize whatever he found to his benefit.

"So, then what do you suggest?" she asked.

Marcus stroked his chin, deep in thought. "You reached out to me mentally once, do you remember?"

"Yes," she admitted. But that had been with the aid of a potion that had taken days to brew. "I could concoct another potion—"

"No, there isn't time."

"Then how?"

He watched her for so long that the hairs on the back of her neck stood on end. Slowly, she began to suspect what he had in mind.

Something terrible.

"No."

"You're afraid, but you shouldn't be," Marcus said.

Miranda felt her eyes narrow. "Then *you* mutilate yourself and use your blood in an arcane ritual. I won't do it. I won't!"

"Will you hear me out?" He crossed his arms, eyeing the beast before them. Something in his stance made her lower her guard and listen. "I know it's a dangerous, risky, and reckless proposition. But think about the alternative. We brew a potion and waste days. Or we can get answers now, via a method I know you can achieve. You already have."

"Oh really? And perhaps you really are an evil agent of Liva after all, and this was your aim from the start? Corner me alone and manipulate me into drawing upon blood magic. Then what? You lure your mother here and have a family reunion?"

"No," Marcus said coldly. "I get this over with so I can return to my life and the people who don't cringe at the sight of me. So, I can discover why my mother corrupted these beasts in the first place and why—now, after all this time—does she seem to want the daemons who live here dead. And perhaps so that I can satisfy the terms of my confinement and get far away from the father who seems to loathe my very existence. How is that for a reason?"

"I'm sorry." She was, oddly enough. The pain in his voice resonated with a part of her she'd thought long since smothered. Not since she'd been a child had she indulged in those petty, angry feelings. But she knew them well.

"But I can't," she insisted. "I told you what it feels like, how it—"

"I never intended for you to use your own blood," Marcus said. He reached for his forearm and peeled off the makeshift bandage. The wound beneath was a glistening patch of bloodied flesh in a perfect square, matching his previous description—exactly four inches. "This time, you can use mine."

"The blood isn't the problem," she said hoarsely. "I prefer to use *honest* magic. Nature. Not this."

Marcus raised an eyebrow. "You're afraid, but I don't think you should be. I can guide you—"

"I thought you didn't use magic?" Miranda couldn't deny the tendril of unease that ran down her spine. Perhaps Liva wasn't the only threat to fear?

His warm, sheepish grin helped to ease some of her discomfort. "I don't," he admitted, serious once again. "As I mentioned before, I am part Raeth. With that heritage comes its own temptations and darkness to counter. I've developed a method to keep my sanity, and I think I can help you in this instance."

He didn't seem ingenuine. If anything, his voice took on a harsher tone that alluded to a struggle roughly equivalent to her internal battle against blood magic. Yet, he claimed to know of a way to combat the fear.

Curiosity alone prompted her to ask, "How?"

"Well..." He extended his hands to her, and she was startled to find that he felt as warm as she did—mortal. "Don't laugh, but it's a fairly simple remedy. You meditate."

Despite his warning, she waited for him to chuckle anyway, but he didn't. Instead, he curled his fingers over hers and inclined his head.

"You trust yourself," he continued, sounding comically calm against the backdrop of a low growl from the direction of the creature waiting just paces away. "And, for the time being anyway, you trust me. Now, close your eyes and listen only to my voice. Nothing else. It isn't the magic you fear, but yourself. For now, that doesn't matter. All that does is reaching out to the mind of another. Focus only on that and ignore the rest."

ELEVEN

Atiernan busied himself with the daily ins and outs of running the fortress, putting all thoughts of the witch and her hybrid cohort from his mind. He took the time to hear the various complaints of the day from his tenants. Then he headed out to survey the barrier in case of another attack from the sentinels. He even stopped by the kitchens to ensure the staff was coping with the added difficulties of feeding two extra mouths, let alone a captive beast.

All in all, he dallied for as long as possible, putting off the final task on his list until the last possible second.

"You're stalling, Atiernan," Peony called disapprovingly from the back of her storeroom.

He'd gone there under the guise of helping her catalog and arrange her ingredients. In reality, he wound up scouring the same shelf of molded roots while trying his damned hardest to prevent his thoughts from cycling back to one particular figure.

Miranda Lightwood.

"Who knows what the two half-breeds have gotten up to amongst themselves," Peony added. "They've had the entire day to plot and conspire. You should tell the cooks to set a place for Liva, because I'm sure she'll arrive before supper." From her tone, Atiernan was sure the mage was only partly joking.

Though she had a point.

He hissed out a sigh. "I should go to the dungeons..."

Yet, several seconds ticked by, and he didn't move a muscle.

"You are worried," Peony surmised. "But not entirely out of concern that they may plot an escape, armed with blood magic. What is truly on your mind?"

He considered lying. Then he quickly reconsidered—Peony would see through him in an instant.

"You didn't see the way she looked at him." His voice rasped, deeper than he was used to. Still, he curled his fist around a root, finding a fitting outlet for his frustration. "She laughed. As if they were damn bosom buddies, to co-opt Beth's phrasing."

"Hah!" Peony threw her head back and laughed, startling him with how genuinely amused she seemed. Then he caught the look she sent his way and realized that the mage wasn't mocking him. She was just as alarmed as he felt. "Well, they are—"

"Don't say it," he snarled. "Miranda is nothing like him."

"But she is," Peony said softly. "If anyone could understand what her life has been like, it is someone who experienced the same hardships. As much as it pains me to admit, that man can relate to her in a way you or I never could."

"Relate to her," Atiernan snarled, tightening his grip on the unfortunate root.

"And more, should they wish," Peony said, her tone scolding. "You do not own her, Atiernan, despite what you may think. Still, I would like to believe that someone with your experience can show a woman things that a man his age can't imagine in his wildest dreams."

He swallowed hard. "It isn't like you to be so vulgar."

"Oh, hush! I've seen it all and done it all—and plenty more. But I warn you, if you want Miranda, you will need to earn her the way any man earns any woman."

"What makes you think I want the woman in any way?"

Peony scoffed and raised a dark eyebrow. "I may be old, but I am not senile yet. Anyone with eyes can see the way you look at her. Frankly, I'm surprised you haven't acted on your lust yet. I know you can be persuasive when you want to be. No woman is a match for a Raeth's charms. Not even a witch—or a hybrid witch."

He frowned at her insinuation. "What makes you think I haven't?"

While not experienced in full, his sexual escapades with Miranda had satisfied him fully. And driven him mad with a craving for more.

"Because you wouldn't be pacing around here, crushing *nern* roots in your fist like a frustrated bull if you had," Peony sniped. She approached him and snatched the mangled stem from his grasp. "Please don't tell me you are threatened by a man not past thirty."

It was an oddly specific number. Too specific.

"How do you know how old the hybrid is?" Atiernan demanded, whirling on the mage. Their conversation the other day had concerned only Liva. Or so Peony had claimed. "Have you spoken with it?"

"No." Peony averted her gaze, fiddling with the root in her grasp. "I... Call it a hunch."

"You are far too intelligent to rely on hunches," he snapped. Then, an answer came to him, perfectly suited to Peony's more devious talents. "No wonder you've been so damn tolerant of Miranda and the hybrid conspiring alone. You've been eavesdropping on them this whole damn time."

"Bah!" Peony huffed. "Eavesdropping sounds so damn childish. Really, Atiernan! I've merely been...cautious. Cautious about our safety and cautious about who we allow within our walls."

"But there is more to it," he realized. "If they were saying anything that truly concerned you, you would be there yourself. Or you would do far more than suggest I go visit."

Instead, the truth was complex and convoluted, which was the perfect match for someone with Peony's sly cunning.

"I haven't been the one stalling—*you* have," Atiernan deduced. "What is it you don't want me to see?"

The mage shook her head in exasperation. "Really, Atiernan—"

"You know me," he said over her. "And you know that if you feigned blissful ignorance of their meeting, I wouldn't race down there to watch them. What is it you aren't saying, old woman?"

She pursed her lips, and he knew he'd hit the nail on the damn head.

"You won't like it," she confessed. "But you are right. I did feel emboldened enough to stall for time."

"Why?" His brain envisioned the worst—Miranda, lying in the dungeon while the hybrid—

"Your male pride can remain intact," Peony scolded. "Nothing is happening between them—romantic at least."

"Then what?"

Peony pursed her lips, revealing the unease she'd managed to disguise until then. "The hybrid is convincing Miranda to enter the thoughts of the beast you captured. The sentinel."

"Why?" But the question was beside the point. He hadn't seen Miranda leave the dungeon all day—and had she come by the storeroom for supplies, he would have noticed.

"Does she mean to conjure a spell from thin air?" he asked, his tone verging on a growl.

"No," Peony said. "The hybrid is convincing her to use blood magic—"

"No." He stormed for the door, seeing red. He barely heard Peony call after him.

"Atiernan, wait!"

"What the hell is wrong with you?" he demanded, facing her, his fangs bared. "Do you aim to let that monster corrupt and conspire right under your fucking nose?"

He wasn't referring to Miranda.

"Do you know how much pain that magic causes her? The torment she's suffered because of it?"

"Yes," Peony said hoarsely. From behind the lenses of her glasses, her gray eyes were wide with genuine concern. "I do. But I also know the greatness she could achieve should she learn to hone her power and not fear it."

"You sound insane, woman—"

"Do you trust her?"

The question threw him off, and he staggered, waiting for a laugh. Peony was more cautious than he could ever be. For her to even propose such a question...

"Of course, I don't," he hissed.

"Well, I think we could," Peony replied, surprising him. "And I don't say that lightly, either. Centuries in hiding, lurking like rats, afraid of our own shadow. Wouldn't you gamble even a kernel of trust if the result is us finally being able to stand on our own? To be safe?"

"And if you've just let an agent of Liva plant her poison right in the heart of our home?"

"Damn, Liva," Peony spat. "It was never her that I was afraid of. It was always *you*. You loved her more than I have seen you love anyone, save your family. Her betrayal nearly broke your soul, and I would rather die than see you go through that pain again. Do you understand me?"

He did, to an extent. Still...

"Miranda isn't a pawn we can use in our game." He entered the hall, aware of the mage's steps in his wake.

"You're right," she called, though he could tell she no longer followed. "She isn't a pawn, but she could be the piece upon which our eventual victory hinges. The true test is if you can trust her to help us. I think we can, but you must let her come into her power on her own. You can't stand in her way, Atiernan."

"Watch me," he growled, though already out of the woman's earshot. Anger fueled his steps, propelling him down the hall at a pace that sent his hair whipping out like a cape.

Damn the mage.

Damn magic.

He stormed into the dungeon with a single-minded focus, barely even noticing the guards he passed on his way.

The sight that greeted him near the creature's cell, however, stopped him dead in his tracks. A horrific scene of Miranda drenched in blood would have been far more welcome than this...

She stood before the hybrid male, their hands clasped, foreheads pressed together. It was such an unexpectedly intimate moment—and evoked none of the darkness he'd come to associate with blood magic.

Contrary to Peony's characterization, they looked *exactly* like lovers. At least until Miranda ran her finger along what looked like an open wound on the man's forearm and popped the bleeding digit into her mouth.

"No!" Atiernan surged forward, blinded by rage and disgust. "What in the name of the gods are you doing—"

"It's alright," the hybrid said, though neither figure looked his way nor broke their embrace. "No harm will come to her."

Contrary to that statement, Atiernan could note plenty of harm already. The slight flush to Miranda's cheeks, for one. The way she swayed despite the hybrid's grasp. Her sudden, agonized gasp as she doubled over with pain.

Atiernan couldn't restrain himself any longer. He lunged, taking her into his arms.

"She's fine," the hybrid insisted. "Just drained. I made sure she didn't exert herself—"

"All you've done is played your part in Liva's web," Atiernan snarled.

The man, Marcus, blinked, but if the words insulted him, he didn't show it. Instead, he cocked an eyebrow, and Atiernan noted that Liva wouldn't have reacted as such. No. Confronted so directly, she would have scratched his eyes out.

"I am not here on her behalf. You can believe that."

"No," Atiernan countered. "You want to know what I believe? That you are no child of mine but an agent of that whore."

Marcus nodded, unaffected. "Fine, then. You want to know what I really am? I am an agent of myself and no one else. Have you thought of that? You were a useful tool to her, playing your role in her game by siring a bastard you didn't even know existed. Don't project your shame onto me."

Atiernan saw red. For a second, the woman in his arms was merely a distraction. No one could insult him as such and get away with it. One thing alone held him back—the soft voice rasping near his ear, "Wait…listen…"

"If it assuages your pride any, know this," Marcus went on coldly. "You weren't the only fool Liva took advantage of, and I am not her only child. Think about that. Imagine the damage they can cause if they aren't freed from her influence, and maybe that will displace your shame of me."

Atiernan said nothing. He just turned, leaving the dungeon with Miranda in his arms. In the brighter lighting of the upper level, she looked dangerously pale, resembling a ghost more than a living woman.

Driven by a renewed sense of urgency, he brought her to the upper floor. Rather than enter the room he gave her, he found himself entering his own chamber. The second he placed her on the bed, she seemed to realize it, stiffening at his scent etched into the sheets.

Her eyes fluttered open, dazed and unfocused. Atiernan couldn't help himself. He cupped her cheek against his palm, surprised when she turned into the touch rather than recoil. That brief moment of reflex affected him unlike anything else.

"Where am I?" she croaked.

"With me. Safe," he added after a heartbeat. Something in her voice made him grudgingly suspect the hybrid had been right. She wasn't in pain. But she didn't seem "fine," either. A sheen of sweat coated her forehead, and he could hear her pulse swishing like mad beneath her skin.

"Look at me," he commanded. "Are you alright?"

"Yes…" she rasped, her eyes unfocused. Suddenly, she grimaced. "No. No. Not alright…"

His throat lurched, and he leaned closer. "Why? Tell me what's wrong."

Her gaze met his, blazing with rage. "Never alright. Not until you die."

TWELVE

Miranda's mind swam in various directions, dangerously disconnected. She couldn't remember up from down or left from right. For a horrifying moment, the entire world was in disarray with no clear meaning. No compass.

But then a voice reached through the dizzying chaos and grabbed her like a hook, yanking her through the wild current toward something cohesive.

"Slow down, witch… Listen to my voice…"

She was lying on a bed. Somewhere safe. Warm.

With someone who held her as though she were made of glass, infinitely fragile. A possession he would never relinquish no matter what force strived to take her from him…

Then she remembered the bastard's name and her sole reason for being in his domain in the first place. As a captive, unloved, and certainly not cared for.

"Where is Marcus?" The question sprung from her lips as she tried to sit up. Her head pounded madly, but as her vision cleared, she couldn't see the man anywhere—though she vaguely recognized that this room, with its familiar plain walls, wasn't remotely near the dungeon. "Where is he? I think… I think I know what he meant."

Contacting the creature's mind had been an experience unlike any Miranda could remember. Marcus' thoughts had been neat and orderly, arranged in a construct that felt alien but familiar. The beast's mind, however, had been a ravaged, vacant place wrought with anger, violence, and impulsive emotions that made her instincts rise to the surface.

She was hungry and wanted to feed—straight from the vein.

She demanded movement.

Freedom.

And…

As her eyes latched onto those of the figure hovering above her, another craving surged, crystal clear. She wanted him, Atiernan.

She needed him dead, or her torment—this unbearable suffering—would never end.

And yet, despite being her sworn enemy, he didn't seem to be in much of a hurry to destroy her first. His voice was uncharacteristically soothing, reaching through the barriers she usually kept up around him.

For a second, she relaxed against his touch, relishing in the husky baritone.

"Did he hurt you?" he asked, stroking the hair from her face. "Can you hear me, Miranda? Answer me!"

"I'm okay," she managed to rasp. "But the sentinel is *not*."

That didn't begin to describe it. So much pain. So much unrestrained anger. Her heart ached even though she recognized that the emotions weren't entirely her own.

"Damn the sentinel," Atiernan snarled. "I'll kill him."

Him. That oddly specific reference warned her that he wasn't referring to the beast locked in a cell.

"No." She placed a hand on his chest before he could move and marveled at the sensations racing through her. Being in the beast's mind had done something to hers. Unleashed something wild and dangerous that made her note and react to all the things broadcasted by the warrior that shouldn't have appealed to her in the slightest.

His strength. His scent. His obvious virility. He would sire strong, beautiful children.

Though why the hell did that suddenly matter?

Groaning, she rubbed her temples and tried to recall her own thoughts and feelings. Hate, yes. Maybe a tiny bit of lust—but nothing more. And confusion. Rationalizing what she'd gleaned from this venture would take time and effort. She would need some healing tea, and perhaps a cup of fortifying broth.

And a nap.

"You shall have it all," Atiernan replied heatedly. Apparently, she'd been thinking out loud. According to his mildly surprised expression, she'd spoken about a lot more than tea.

Which gave a whole new context to his reply.

Miranda blanched. "I need you to leave me alone—"

"I'm not going any-damn-where," Atiernan snarled over her. His tone made her shudder. It was one he'd rarely used at her directly—typically only during the times the sentinel managed to breach the perimeter. The low rasp of a blood-thirsty warrior. "What the hell were you thinking? Using blood magic on a whim! To enter the mind of a goddamn beast?"

"Why?" she asked harshly. "Because I am too weak?"

If he thought so, he definitely wouldn't think her a suitable mate—not that his preference mattered.

"Or because you were worried that a taste of dark magic would tip me over the edge?" she added. "I'd suddenly try and destroy you all?"

"No," Atiernan said with surprising calmness. "I was worried about you. That you might hurt yourself."

His fingers raked through her hair, smoothing the strands from her face. While compassion was not necessarily a dominant trait, it heralded fairness that would make him a good provider and father…

"My head," Miranda croaked.

"Tell me what happened," Atiernan insisted. "It might help you to settle back within your own thoughts. Take your time."

As if he knew a fraction of what this felt like. Then she remembered that he did. Raeths were among the few accomplished at mind delving, seeing into the deepest intentions of another. Such a skill would make him an excellent fighter, and a very generous lover—

"It might help if you don't think so much out loud," the leader warned.

Though from his tone, he didn't seem to mind her sudden impulsive honesty. It was how the sentinels lived. Raw and open with each other, no matter the context or risk.

To lie and deceive was to give in to weakness. They could not tolerate an ounce of weakness—such flaws were immediately sought out and destroyed. Strength was the only way in which their kind would thrive. Physical prowess was only part of it. Strength of character. Strength of mind. Honor to a fault.

"I don't think the sentinels are evil," Miranda managed to say. Forming that lone coherent thought seemed to be the catalyst needed to help clear her mind of the recollections that weren't her own. She could think clearly again. Somewhat. "They *aren't* evil," she clarified. "They are terrified. They believe killing you is the only way to save their people, and they will not stop until they do."

"That sounds pretty damn evil to me," Atiernan replied. Perched beside her, he resembled a creature far more fearful than any sentinel.

Miranda shook her head. "There is more to it than that. They feel as though they have no choice. Their lands are dying. Children are failing to be born. They cannot survive such strife for much longer."

The cause of their suffering, however, had been no mystery at all.

"It's Liva," she added. "She planted a tree in the sentinels' ancestral lands. For years, it protected them, shielded them, and provided sustenance but now… It's corrupting the land. Soon, the resulting blight will kill them all—" She broke off as Atiernan stood, lifting her into his arms as though she weighed nothing. "What are you doing?"

"Getting you that tea," he brusquely replied. "On second thought…" He placed her back down with an unreadable expression. "There is something else that could restore your strength a hell of a lot faster."

Miranda watched, puzzled, but all he did was cock his head.

"What do you mean…" Oh. She finally recognized the symbolic gesture for what it was, and a mixture of fear and conflicted gratitude fluttered in her belly. "I don't know if—"

"I won't force you," Atiernan insisted. "I won't waste my breath trying to convince you, either. Just know that I do not practice charity. Anything I give you, I expect to receive repayment for. Especially this."

Oddly enough, reminding her of the transactional relationship was the right play. It made it far easier to make yet another bargain with him, rather than denying how her mouth watered or that sitting upright was a struggle in her current state.

As if sensing her acquiesce before she even voiced it, he moved to stand before her and crouched, bringing his throat within her reach.

"Come, witch," he taunted. "Take what you need from me."

His fangs descended as he spoke, and he brought his wrist to his mouth and bit down.

Miranda hated how her mouth watered even more at the sight of the dark, rich beads of scarlet that dribbled over his golden skin. In the end, Atiernan merely coaxed her with a softly murmured command of, "Drink," before she lowered her head and sealed her lips around the pinprick wounds.

It should have been criminal for such a taboo substance to taste so damn good. She moaned as the unique flavor met her tongue, and deep down, she knew that Atiernan, or a desire to recover her strength, wasn't what drove her to keep drinking.

Just the sinful act of deciphering a nuanced aspect of this man who seemed equally eager to discover everything there was to know about her.

Still, she let herself indulge for only a second before pulling back, licking her lips clean.

"Good," Atiernan praised with a raspy chuckle. "I shall take my payment later. For now, let's share your concerns with someone who can tell us what they mean."

Minutes later, she found herself in Peony's storeroom, being shoved onto a wooden chair while the mage rushed around, cramming herbs into a teapot.

"Oh, this does explain much," the woman prattled, digesting what little Miranda had managed to relay. "Much indeed. And yet, it presents far more questions. Why now? And the sentinels' attacks have not started recently, out of the blue."

"They have been attacking our kind for years," Atiernan pitched in from where he stood nearby, his arms crossed. "With every passing one, their viciousness has only increased. That doesn't sound like a dying, tortured people to me."

"It isn't that simple," Miranda said, cradling her aching head with one hand. It still took so much effort to decipher the jumble of information running through her brain. Only when Peony finally set a mug of steaming tea in front of her could she actually string together a coherent reply. "The land hasn't failed overnight, but gradually. Over decades, in fact. Only a few sentinels were driven to react at first, but now they feel they have no choice. Inaction now means instant death. There is no other way for them. Or so Gulurg believes."

Her tongue struggled with the unfamiliar syllables.

"That's the name of the creature in the dungeon."

Atiernan scoffed. Peony, however, seemed more thoughtful than dismissive.

"And yet, they have such a clear cause as to the source behind their pain," she remarked, stroking her chin. "It could be a tragic reality, or a very convincing story."

"One fed to them," Atiernan pitched in. "It wouldn't be the first time she pitted two races against each other with violence and lies."

His tone implied a dark history Miranda knew she would need to delve into later. For now, she took another sip of tea, finally calmed enough to rationally convey more of what she'd learned.

"It isn't their story, however," she admitted. "All they know is that Atiernan is the source of their pain. It's like a mantra running through their head repeatedly, as if planted there. I don't think they even realize who the true cause of their troubles is."

"Then how do you know?" Atiernan asked.

"Because I saw their sacred tree," Miranda admitted, still marveling at the image of the towering, sprawling tree at the center of their homeland. "It was a light wood tree, much like the one planted in the holy grove of Hazel's Way. Nearly thirty years ago, our tree was destroyed, and, at the same time, theirs began to decay and mutate. Any creature who fed on its fruit began to mutate as well. Year after year, it's been getting worse."

"But why now?" Atiernan wondered. "What is the link between them? Perhaps those trees just reached the end of their life cycles—"

"No," Miranda said softly. "Twenty-eight years ago, I was born. So was Marcus. In fact, I think we both drew our first breath on the same night."

It was an alarming thought to consider. After years of believing she was a lonely, corrupted outcast, she learned that someone else shared the same heritage. The same age. The same birthday, perhaps down to the very minute.

"How?" Atiernan swore, his eyes wide. "Are you—"

"She isn't a child of that woman, I can assure you," Peony interjected. "But yes… I understand now. A very interesting conundrum indeed."

"My birth destroyed the light wood tree," Miranda explained. "I always thought it was proof of my corruption —my damned birth."

"But what if it merely served as the catalyst to a devious plan set in motion centuries prior by one malicious little witch?" Peony nodded at her own proposal, her eyes gleaming behind the foggy lenses of her glasses. "Oh yes, it was a clever plan. Very clever indeed. The meticulous planning, the timing…"

"Will someone enlighten me?" Atiernan demanded, an eyebrow raised.

"Marcus believes that he was conceived when you knew Liva intimately," Miranda said, hating how the phrasing sounded out loud. She pictured Atiernan with such a woman, doing the acts necessary to create a child.

And shuddered.

"But that is unlikely, if not preposterous," Atiernan said. "No one can live for centuries without… A sacrifice. This man claims to be younger than thirty—"

"Yes, oh yes!" Peony clapped her hands though her expression wasn't gleeful in the slightest. "That cunning bitch. I understand perfectly now. One can exist but not technically be 'living.'"

She raced off toward a shelf and began to noisily rummage through the assorted materials stacked on top of it.

"Care to explain?" Atiernan remarked.

"Ah! Like so—" Peony returned with a box of what looked like black rocks in tow. Gingerly, she placed it in the center of the table and prodded one of the misshapen lumps with her finger. "These are the seeds of a *Mahop* plant. A beautiful, thriving vine that, once fully grown, can choke the life out of an entire army at once. Just like that."

"I don't follow," Atiernan said.

"Then *listen*. *Mahop* seeds require very specific conditions to grow. I have had these seeds for decades, and even if I were to plant them now in my garden, they wouldn't take root. You need the right soil, the right lighting conditions, and of course, fresh blood—"

"I think I need to regulate what you bring into my manor more, Peony."

"Bah! Will you hush and let me speak?" The mage planted her hands on her hips and seemed to grow inches taller in an instant. Atiernan bowed his head respectfully, and she soldiered on with an indignant sigh. "Despite its rather sensitive and delicate nature, it does not matter how long I keep these seeds in a box, shoved on the back shelf of a very dusty storeroom. Be it tomorrow or a thousand years from now—the second I place them in the required conditions, they will sprout roots and grow. It does not matter that, for now, they are just useless bits of clutter. The dangerous plant within still exists, though not technically alive."

Atiernan's eyes widened as understanding dawned on him. "That cunning bitch."

"Yes," Peony agreed. "She carried your son, alright. Then she hid him right under your nose for centuries where he remained, in existence but not quite alive."

"In the light wood tree. Until me," Miranda said hoarsely. "My birth triggered his. But why?"

"That is what we must figure out," Peony said gravely. "Nothing good, I am sure. Damn, I just rearranged my bookshelves, too. Where did I put that one tome of ancient prophecies—"

"It... Marcus, said he wasn't Liva's only child," Atiernan said, his expression constricted. "He said there were others."

"Well, I think it's time that you and I formally met this son of yours," Peony said. "The nature of his birth changes everything. If he truly is as young as he claims, then there is no way he can understand the true context of his conception. Or your absence from his life."

"Or, this could be yet another trick meant to misdirect our anger," Atiernan suggested. "Why trust any of it?"

"Because I did this," Miranda said, though she could barely speak. "This is all my fault. If Liva planned something… I am the one who set it all into motion."

"And that puts your mother's actions into far greater clarity," Peony said, nodding. "Oh yes. Why else would a witch from such a hallowed clan consult with a daemon for power? Unless…"

"What are you saying?" Atiernan demanded.

"Think of it," Peony began. "A young witch from that coven of Hazel, approached by an ancestor long thought dead. A woman who claimed to be the very founder of her coven and offered to share the secret behind her success and immortality."

"She led your mother to Azareal," Atiernan said to Miranda directly. "She convinced her to make a deal."

Peony sighed. "And through that deal, a child was born. A child who in turn released Liva's own unborn infant, sealed for centuries within the tree the witches had worshiped and protected for generations."

"It sounds like her," Atiernan admitted. "Coyly manipulating those in her orbit to do her bidding, whether they want to or not."

"But why?" Miranda asked, feeling more hopeless than confused. "Why go through all of this trouble? Why me? Why Marcus?"

"I'm afraid the answer to that eludes us still," Peony said. "If we are to have any hope of stopping the woman at her own game, we must act fast. Knowing her, nothing good can come from these actions. Nothing good at all."

Including the children created by her twisted meddling. Miranda felt her shoulders slump as the true horror of her conception dawned on her. Her mother hadn't merely been a callous woman hellbent on her own power. She'd been tricked by an ancient witch with aims of her own. She'd been manipulated by a daemon and saddled with a child she never wanted.

To what end?

Deep down, she knew that she never wanted to find out.

***

"I'M FINE," Miranda insisted for the hundredth time. Those two words had become a mantra, though for a reason she could have never fathomed even a few days ago.

Atiernan, acting as her nursemaid, was an outcome of her scheming that even Liva most likely hadn't foreseen.

The man seemed determined to coddle her since their unsettling conversation in the storeroom. At first, she couldn't deny that his attentions hadn't been entirely unwanted.

He carried her back into her room and ran a bath infused with the scents of honey and lavender. Then he arranged to have more tea brought up to her, along with an appetizing meal and a towering bowl of fresh, exotic fruits.

All of it seemed like something fit for a queen. She might have even tolerated it.

Until the man revealed his intentions to not only pamper her, but bathe her as well.

"You are exhausted," he replied scathingly to her refusal. "In this state, you're more likely to fall asleep in the water than wash. Let me help you. Now lift your arms."

His unnervingly gentle tone was what shocked her into complying—nothing else. Before she could even think through the consequences of what she'd done, her dress was on the floor, and her body was once again in Atiernan's arms.

"I am fine," she insisted merely to salvage her pride. "You don't need to coddle me like some traumatized little girl."

"I am not coddling you," the warrior replied, all while lowering her into the steaming, perfumed water of a bathtub large enough to fit three other women in addition to her. "I am… Protecting you."

She didn't miss how he seemed to fish for that word. Still, she marveled at it anyway.

"I don't need your protection," she said.

She didn't, however, disregard how odd it was that he was willing to make it available to her. An ancient daemon warrior extending his protection to a witch from the coven of Hazel. It seemed a lot like…

Well, like history repeating itself.

"Did you offer Liva your protection?" she asked. So much of his history with the witch was still shrouded in mystery. Yet, the man had learned nearly all there was to know about her.

"Once," he admitted. "I believed she needed it—a mistake I've spent the last thousand or so years paying for."

"Tell me what happened."

He sighed. "It was near the height of the great war between daemons and witches. I'm sure you learned their version already?"

She nodded, though internally, she marveled at his casual admittance at having been present for an event so long in the past. Clearing her throat, she prepared to recite the tale as young witches learned it.

"Once, everyone was human. The earth was dying. A group of women did their best to find a way to save their people. In the process, they became witches—"

"And some became daemons," Atiernan replied. "I'm sure they gloss over the how and why. Those original witches sacrificed the youngest and most virtuous among them to derive their power. In other words…"

"Blood magic," Miranda hoarsely supplied. Did she believe him? So much about what was taught in the coven had already turned out to be a lie. Why should the story of their origins be any different?

"In doing so," Atiernan went on, "they created a rift that corrupted those responsible. Some became witches, and others took on the various traits of what would become the daemon races. The witches considered themselves more worthy of being the stewards of the mortal realm, so they banished my kind to another world they deemed Hell and enslaved us for centuries."

"Then the daemons rebelled," Miranda continued. "And you rescued Liva from her own coven."

That part he had already revealed.

"Yes," he said. "Or, as you put it, I offered her my 'protection.'"

"But you so eagerly offer it again?"

"You are not her," Atiernan scolded as if reading her mind. In the same instance, he crouched behind her and ran his fingers through her hair, parting the tangled strands. The action felt so surreal and soothing that she feared she'd gone insane.

"What if I am," she rasped, unwilling to let the subject drop. "A more devious and cunning and corrupted creature than she could ever hope to be?"

"Bullshit," Atiernan replied with confidence, catching her off guard.

She craned her neck to watch him, alarmed to find that stroking her hair wasn't a random impulse on his part. At his side was a bottle of liquid she suspected might have been shampoo, procured with the sole intention of being lathered within his massive hands and worked into her scalp while she watched, mouth agape.

"How can you be so sure?" she asked. Though, if this was how he treated all his evil witch lovers, perhaps said title wasn't all that bad.

Until she remembered that Liva had arranged for her birth with the sole purpose of using her to trigger the release of another hybrid, centuries in the making.

"Because… I'm sure we would have mated by now if you were," Atiernan said. He seemed surprised by the words as much as she was. Though he didn't pause in his ministrations.

Miranda couldn't help but relax as he worked the lather through her hair, triggering a rich scent that instantly soothed her throbbing headache.

Mirthwood.

"I hope you plan to elaborate," she said tiredly. Already, her eyelids were starting to drift shut.

"Liva never hesitated in her pursuit of me," Atiernan replied, his voice gentle as if to further coax her into a dizzy half-slumber. "She expressed her interest the very moment I took her. I managed to restrain myself out of honor. Even back then, sex out of marriage was considered taboo. A sin. But she was persistent…"

He trailed off, and Miranda had an unwelcome mental image of him picturing that night in his head. Over and over again.

Was this jealousy? Whatever the name for the feeling itching through her chest was, she didn't enjoy it one damn bit.

"You think I can't be evil because I am not trying to seduce you at every turn?"

It was an interesting concept, but Atiernan's laugh only confused her further.

"No. I meant that, from the start, Liva only wanted something from me. My sex. My blood. My power. I was just too foolish to see it. You, on the other hand, cringe at the sight of me. You have yet to admit that my body and touch give you pleasure. You withhold yourself from me at every turn, even though I can tell your body wouldn't mind the experience. You have your own goals and morals. You haven't made yourself a caricature of what you think I want to appeal to me."

His voice was so damn soft, as if his lips were mere inches from her ear. Still, he worked, lulling her body into a false sense of security. Surely, any minute, he would wrap his hands around her throat and do what he should have done the day he brought her here.

"You are too afraid of yourself to give a damn about seducing me," the warrior went on. "I know cunning. I know seduction. You have very little of either."

Amused, she raised an eyebrow. "You don't think me to be cunning?"

"No." His voice resonated down her spine in a dangerous whisper. He was even closer, his chest braced against her shoulders. "To be cunning, one must be a good liar, which you are not."

"I lied about being a full-blooded witch," she pointed out. "You didn't see through me then."

"You never lied. You merely assumed the identity I had already suspected. In fact, I think if I asked you outright back then, you would have come clean. Or I would have seen directly through your act. Liva is a very convincing liar. Few could match her skill."

"You wouldn't have believed I was a hybrid then, anyway," Miranda pointed out. "You said such a creature couldn't exist. Don't you remember?"

And maybe she was still bitter about that. For a man to go from scoffing at the mere idea of a hybrid, to bathing one... Well, it seemed a change far too drastic to be realistic.

Perhaps he was the cunning one in this scenario?

"I said it," he admitted. "And, I can't deny that I wish I had been right. The pain you've been through, I can't imagine it. Never. A mother should love her child unconditionally, not hurt her. Use her. Torment her."

His characterization made her flinch, sending water sloshing at the rim of the tub.

"I was not so helpless. I even rebelled against my mother once."

"Oh?" He sounded so gentle, still, as if he expected her rebellion to extend to something as simple as refusing to take the trash out when told.

"Yes. I disobeyed her biggest rule, and I used blood magic on my own," she confessed. "Without her coercion or command."

"What did you do?" His fingers stilled. Did he suspect something horrific like a rampage of death and murder, the likes of which could only be caused by a scorned half-breed?

"I contacted my father," Miranda admitted, an anti-climactic crime when all was said and done. "With what little I knew of him, I was able to reach out to his mind."

"And?"

She shivered. His mind had been more alien and feral than the sentinel, though he had only tolerated her presence for an instant before locking her out.

"I didn't get much. No actual words addressed to me directly either, just a fragment of a thought."

"Which was?" Atiernan had finished his lather. Now, he used his cupped hands to apply water to her hair, rinsing it.

She hesitated. It had been so very long ago, and she'd almost succeeded in blocking out the recollection completely.

"You can tell me," Atiernan said. "His ilk cannot harm you here."

"It didn't harm me, per se," she said. "It merely clarified what I already knew. When I reached out to the daemon I believe to be my father, his first thought wasn't confusion or even alarm. It was…disgust. *Vermin,* he thought. *Should be dead.*"

Her voice broke. A sob came from nowhere, and within seconds she was hunched forward, crying openly. The sounds… They weren't like the smothered whimpers from her childhood. They echoed, broken and howling and filled with so much pain.

The worst part of breaking down in front of a daemon wasn't bawling her eyes out in a tepid bathtub, either. It was that, rather than stare on in shock, or turn away, he…

Climbed inside the tub to hold her against his chest as if nearness to him alone could soothe her pain. He was still fully clothed, the damp material of his shirt the only barrier separating him from her bare skin.

"Hush," he murmured against her temple. "I know it hurts."

"It wasn't fair!" A broken laugh escaped her next, and the tears fell harder. "How was it that a monster like him couldn't even bear to speak to me? I am *that* cursed. That broken—"

"No." Atiernan shifted her to face him and stroked her damp hair away, leaving nothing to obscure her view of him. "I know Azareal personally, and I can assure you that he is no paragon of virtue. The bastard is the lowest form of daemon, eagerly used by the likes of Liva as a servant. If he considered you vermin, I would take it as the highest form of compliment."

"I know some of the horrors he's responsible for," Miranda admitted—many crimes written about in mortal history books as freak acts of nature or horrific criminal acts committed by a few deranged humans. The truth was that, in exchange for power, even mortals made deals with Vaer daemons, the likes of Azrael. In return, the creatures relished in the chaos sowed by greed.

And yet, he hadn't seemed to gloat in the acknowledgment from a daughter bred to a witch. Even a bastard as despicable as him had seemed horrified by her mere existence.

Almost as if…

"I was meant to die." She sat bolt upright, feeling her brain race with the same unsteady wildness it had after she'd entered the sentinel's mind.

Suddenly, so much seemed clear to her, and she could barely spit the words out in a coherent order.

"My mother wasn't meant to keep me. She should have killed me."

In fact, on the very spot of sin that horrified the witches of Hazel to this day.

"The crones would have wanted her to. I'm sure they demanded it, but she didn't—"

"What are you saying?" Atiernan demanded.

She faced him, overwhelmed by the possibility forming in her own head. If it held any water, it served that Liva wasn't quite so infallible.

And yet, their situation was far more precarious than they could have imagined.

"I need to see Marcus and Peony," she said in a rush. "I'll explain it all then."

"You need sleep first," Atiernan warned. "Then you can speak to them. But to explain what?"

"Why I wasn't meant to live."

THIRTEEN

With the increasing sentinel attacks wreaking havoc on his people, Atiernan could admit that it took far more than a little violence, doubt, and magic to unsettle him.

Combine all three within the package of a slender woman, however, and the resulting creature just might have been his match.

Miranda, the witch, seated across from him, her hair unbound and damp from her bath, unsettled him in a way he hadn't felt ever. She aroused emotions in him he'd thought long since buried. She made him feel things he didn't think were capable of being felt by a daemon.

She made him recall the twisted remnants of a physical state he hadn't embodied in too many years to list. She made him feel human.

And humans were prone to the one emotion he couldn't risk feeling ever again—fear.

"Okay, we are here," Peony said with a hasty glance over her shoulder. "I suggest you explain the meaning behind this."

Atiernan knew the mage was just as uneasy as he was. Despite her penchant for eavesdropping, it seemed as though the woman wasn't quite comfortable with having two half-breeds within touching distance of each other. Miranda sat on one end of the table, and the hybrid Marcus lingered by the door. Only Atiernan stood in between him and the witch—a position that wasn't by coincidence.

"Speak," Peony commanded.

"I think my mother was meant to kill me at birth," Miranda began, her eyes downcast, and her skin so pale he itched to feel her head for a sign of a fever. "It would have been demanded, in fact, by the coven elders after the destruction of the light wood tree. Our customs call for those of such corruption to be slain on holy ground, so that their blood might replenish the favor the gods had revoked. In this case, that would have meant the grounds of the lightwood tree."

"Describe this place," Peony insisted.

Miranda leaned back in her chair, her jaw tight with concentration. "It is a grove in the heart of the forest we call home. A protected area, guarded by strong magic. Only the highest-ranked members of the coven can access the tree directly. Where it once stood is now charred, blackened earth."

"Ah, but right after your birth, I'm sure that land would have been a direct conduit to our Marcus. Fresh blood dripped into the waiting maw of a newborn baby Raeth. Oh, dear." Peony clucked her tongue and began to pace.

"I don't understand," Atiernan spoke up. "If Liva did seal her son in the sacred tree, and he was freed with the birth of a half-daemon. Why would a sacrifice matter?"

If anything, he suspected Liva would prefer two half-breeds to fund her twisted magic rather than one.

"You forget," Peony eyed him, chewing on her lower lip. "Raeths are not born—not with the gifts that have cursed us to live the life we have. They are made. With a sacrifice. You remember when Beth was born? That day I fed her a few drops of my own blood so that she would quickly learn to control her hunger."

Atiernan felt his eyes narrow as he finally understood just what the mage hinted at. Then he inspected the man who claimed to be his son. Even from here, he noted the absence of fangs, and he had offered Miranda his blood rather than take hers.

"You aren't afflicted with bloodlust," he deduced, noting the almost mortal-like pallor of the man's skin. "You haven't killed, at least not during a feeding—"

"I have never fed," Marcus declared, his chin in the air. "And I don't plan to."

"And that, I suspect, has put a wrench in your mother's grand plans," Peony deduced, sounding almost gleeful. "If Miranda had been sacrificed at birth, such pure blood imbibed with both the power of a witch and a daemon would have awoken your instincts before you could even think to control them. I am sure you have lived a mortal lifespan, yes?"

Marcus nodded.

"Well then, imagine if you had tasted blood from the first second you drew breath? You would have craved it with the same instinctive need that you crave fresh air. You would have fed on hundreds to sate such hunger. Thousands. By now, you would have been like…"

She trailed off, and Atiernan didn't miss the wary glance she shot in his direction.

"You would have been like us," he said. "Raeths who feed on fresh blood—who kill while feeding—can extend their own life with every mortal one they steal."

"And how many have you stolen?" Marcus demanded. "You shun me like I'm a monster, but what about *you*, Atiernan the Blood Warrior? Spare me your dramatic tale of strife and woe. I've already heard it—you've killed thousands. More than I'm sure you even recall. Regardless of how I was born, my mother abandoned me afterward. I was found on the side of the road by mortal farmers and taken in as though I were their own. The problem? Even as a child, I knew the truth about my parentage. The earliest thought I can remember is the prevalent knowledge of what I am and who sired me."

"Spending so long existing and yet not alive would impart some knowledge, even in an unborn mind," Peony suspected.

Atiernan didn't buy it. "And you never met your mother once? Yet you seem well versed in her chosen magic."

"I never said I hadn't met her," Marcus countered.

"And he hasn't used blood magic," Miranda pitched in. "Only me."

"When I was five years old, Liva came to me, into the home I'd been adopted into," Marcus continued. "She took one look at me and said that nature had failed me, but I could right its wrong. Then she gave me a knife and enthralled my parents to present their throats to me so I could slice them open myself."

Miranda gasped, horrified, but Atiernan wasn't. That sounded like Liva, ironically similar to the method she'd used to awaken his own Raeth instincts. In that case, a seemingly willing witch maiden had cut her own throat before him.

"And did you?" he asked.

The man scoffed. "No. As it turns out, I didn't inherit your knack for killing and violence. I couldn't harm the woman I'd learn to call Mother. So, Liva did it for me and commanded me to drink her blood—"

"Gods above," Miranda croaked, lurching to her feet. She looked disgusted, with one hand pressed against her mouth. Atiernan wasn't fooled by the display, however.

Her sympathy wasn't directed solely to the unnamed woman in that sad tale—but to him. Marcus. She understood his pain on a visceral level. One even Atiernan couldn't comprehend.

Liva hadn't killed *his* birth mother to awaken his instincts, just nameless witch peasants tarred with the title of an enemy in the heat of a vicious war. He had rationalized their deaths then as being for the greater good. Only now, years later, could he mourn for their loss.

And despise himself for being the cause of such suffering.

"I didn't drink," Marcus continued. "So she left me there in a house covered in blood, with two rotting bodies. Do you want to know what happened next? It wasn't until nearly a week later that a neighbor came by and found me. A local witch saw the news report and suspected what might have happened. It took her five years to track me down in an orphanage. She alone raised me after that, and *she* taught me about magic. Not Liva."

"A likely story," Atiernan surmised. "Who was this woman?"

"Someone you will never meet if I can help it," Marcus replied.

"Oh?" Anger wasn't what Atiernan felt coil in his chest. Alarm perhaps? He might have said those words to anyone he believed for a second would cause those he loved harm.

"We can leave the threats aside for now," Peony said gently. Atiernan was surprised as she came to stand between them, her hands held in a placating gesture.

"You believe him," he suspected.

The mage had enough tact to ignore him. For now.

But Atiernan knew her enough to know when she was suspicious and when her interest was piqued. First Miranda, now his supposed son. What next? She would adopt the sentinel in the dungeon under her protection as well?

"Atiernan told me that you believe there are other children like yourself," Peony continued. "Is that true?"

Marcus crossed his arms, his head cocked in an expression Atiernan recognized—it was like looking into a goddamn mirror.

"He won't tell us anything," he said. "Not without convincing."

"Or assurances that we won't hurt them," Miranda pitched in. "They may be Liva's children. That doesn't condemn them to death, does it?"

Atiernan said nothing. Peony, like always, had far more tact.

"Should they cause no harm, I suppose not," the mage mused. "But therein lies the hard question anyone has yet to ask. For what purpose would Liva conceive her children? I am sure each has a father as carefully chosen as Atiernan, if not him."

"There are different fathers," Marcus admitted. "Fortunately, I am the only one I know of with Raeth blood."

"Others..." Peony tutted again and took off toward another part of her storeroom. "I need my tomes!" she cried. "Where did I put the damned things?"

"This will take her a while," Atiernan suspected, sensing the mage's true aim was to stall. What had Peony suspected that he hadn't?

Nothing good.

In the meantime, she had left Atiernan to salvage this mess of a meeting. Frankly, he had no idea how. Rather than face the male hybrid, he focused his attention on Miranda.

"You look pale," he said, startled by how rough his voice sounded. "That magic took more out of you than you admitted. You need rest."

"I'm fine," she said. Once again, her lack of skill with lying was on full display.

He could only suspect how exhausted she truly was. Yet she seemed determined to remain on her feet, within earshot of anything important. Azareal was a Vaer daemon, and they were renowned for their intelligence and hunger for knowledge. And their preference for striking bargains. No wonder.

"There is one thing I still don't understand," Miranda said, her gaze inward. "If she knew. My mother or Liva... If either of them knew what the other planned. If so, why not kill me herself?"

"Your usefulness to her probably passed once you aged," Marcus suggested.

"Or," Atiernan growled, inching forward. "Liva hasn't ceased her attempts to harm you. In fact, she sent the very creature who requires your blood right to you."

He grabbed her arm, pulling her behind him with a ferocity that had her gasping.

"What are you doing—"

"You never explained why exactly you've sought me out now, daemon," Atiernan said, his gaze on the male hybrid. "Why now? And why at the exact moment she happens to be on my property? You've had nearly a decade since you reached maturity to find me. Why now, when the sentinel attacks have reached an inflection point? What is it you truly want?"

Marcus laughed, an eyebrow raised. "To be honest with you, I don't actually know. Perhaps I wanted to lay my eyes on the man who sired me? Perhaps I wanted to see if there was some small fraction of humanity left within you that would spur you to help me fight Liva's evil. Maybe I simply wanted to meet my father so that I could finally know if you were worth mourning or not. Thankfully, in any case, I have found my answer."

"Atiernan." Miranda's voice scratched against his ear. She was worried. "I think you should listen to him—"

"No," he bellowed. "I know what I should do, and that is keep you far away from him. He will return to his realm the second you can muster the right spell. Do not argue with me."

He spun on his heel, dragging the woman after him by her arm. To his shock, she didn't resist, keeping pace with his long strides.

As they neared the doorway, Peony's voice rang out.

"You, hybrid—no, my apologies, *Marcus*. Marcus, you will stay."

Atiernan hissed through his teeth. He could smell her meddling thoughts from a mile away. "Peony—"

"Go tend to your witch before she faints on my floor," the mage huffed. "Marcus, come. We have much to discuss, and I am not tall enough to reach these tomes. This way."

"Don't make me regret your scheming, woman," Atiernan called back, though he didn't stay to see if the mage cared to heed his request.

The second he left the storeroom, Miranda became his sole focus. Peony hadn't been exaggerating—she looked liable to faint any second. Heedless of his nearby guards, he pulled her against his chest, cradling her body in his arms.

She attempted to resist. "I am fine—"

"Save your arguments, witch," he told her, heading for the stairs. "You are still my captive, under my control, in *my* domain."

In other words, she was his. He intended to treat his newest possession the way he did everything else under his purview —with obsessive care and attention to detail.

"I'm taking you to bed," he said, though he didn't need to explain himself. "You will sleep. Then I will feed you a hearty meal you won't refuse."

"And then we will talk," Miranda said softly.

Atiernan groaned. Was every woman in his life determined to thwart him at every turn? At least her remaining defiance warned that what afflicted her wasn't anything worse than exhaustion. For now.

"Talk about what?"

"My mother," Miranda replied, though her voice sounded softer. A glance downward revealed that her eyes were already shut, with those long lashes settling against her cheeks. "I need to see her."

A request he would pretend not to hear.

"What you need now, witch, is rest, food, and…"

He had enough respect for her pride to leave the last thing she would require unspoken. Though in his head, it echoed loud and clear.

The witch needed him more than she realized. He would ensure that no harm came to her. Not from his so-called son. Not from Liva.

Not even from herself.

FOURTEEN

Miranda stirred to awareness with delicious images of Atiernan floating inside her head. Had it been a dream, or had the man really bathed her as though she were a porcelain doll?

The thought brought a smile to her lips that she promptly smothered. *No.* Letting her guard down around the daemon wouldn't do any good. She would need to remain strong. If he attempted any further actions designed to sneak past her defenses, she had to resist him at every turn. She needed to…

Sleep beside him, wrapped in his arms, apparently. His nearness had a certain feel, his scent unmistakable even while her brain shrugged off the remnants of sleep. The man was more potent than the most devious poisons, sinking through her veins and evading every wall and barrier she had in place.

"Sleep," he commanded before she even opened her eyes. "You will have plenty of time to wallow in despair later. How terrible a witch you are to lie willingly beside a daemon."

She could have ignored the taunt and feigned sleep. She certainly felt exhausted enough to drift off for another hour at least. Something in his tone made her rise to the challenge and peel her eyes open just enough to view his face.

Gods above, the man was beautiful. The kind of beauty no one could deny, enemy or foe. His voice was just as dangerous, rasping through her skin and resonating in the bones beneath. He had her facing him, with only a silken pillow between them. One of his hands lurked just beyond the reach of her cheek. As if he'd been stroking her while she'd been asleep and stopped himself the second he sensed her awake.

The image terrified her. Almost as much as the fact that she hadn't flinched away from him, shrieking.

"You have a strange method of captivity, daemon," she said tiredly. "I think I preferred being left in your dungeon to rot."

"Only because there you could hide from what both you and I sense, witch."

His tone was far too deep, spurring her pulse into a maddening rhythm.

"Oh? And what is that?"

His eyes seemed to sparkle, bathed in moonlight. It had to be very late or very early—either way, far too much time to waste given everything on their plate. Liva, the sentinel, and now Marcus and her mother's motives. Still, Atiernan could demand attention no matter the current dilemmas vying for someone's focus. The man was that damn magnetic. That powerful.

"You know what." His gaze cut down to her mouth and his own tongue slipped along his lower lip in a careless motion that made her breath catch. "You know that nothing short of your precious gods descending from on high will stop me from tying you down… And forcing some sustenance down your throat. Come."

He sat up, tugging her with him. Miranda was alarmed to find that food had already been brought to her room and waited, steaming, on a table nearby.

She attempted to stand, but Atiernan moved first, blocking her path to the table with his bulk alone. With unmistakable concern, he took his time preparing a plate for her from the assorted platters of meats and vegetables. When he finally placed a serving onto the bed beside her, Miranda could only gape at the extravagant spread arranged on a priceless porcelain plate.

"I thought you were showing off before," she admitted. "But do you really eat this lavishly every night?"

Atiernan raised an eyebrow as if her awe confused him. Apparently, roasted duck, braised vegetables, and fruits from every corner of the world were a mainstay here in his fortress.

"My people need food. I strive to bring them any and everything they could possibly desire. Your shock should be reserved for the cooks, who have free rein to serve what they like. I take it from your reaction that witches prefer humbler fair."

She nodded, though she still accepted the fork he offered her next. Then she cautiously sampled a bit of cooked meat and moaned at the taste. "Only on banquet nights would they be served something a fraction as elaborate as this," she confessed. "Those nights were few and far between. Perhaps a handful a year. Otherwise, the mess halls served simple meals composed of fresh vegetables. Cabbage cakes. Fruit pies. Porridge. Rarely any meat."

"So pious you witches are," Atiernan remarked while sitting beside her. "I'm sure there was some rule of never wishing for more than leaves and roots, lest you provoke the wrath of your gods."

"Something like that," Miranda replied.

The truth was, the food he scoffed at was considered far too good for the likes of her. She had been given gruel, bread, and whatever scraps the kitchen workers felt like tossing her way every now and again. Never did she partake in the banquets. Sin required no celebration.

"I've upset you."

She shook her head. "No, I was just… Remembering."

"It doesn't seem as though you enjoy those memories."

She filled the silence by eating her fill, and Atiernan would refill her glass or add more servings to her plate. Miranda figured she could have refused. Perhaps shock alone rendered her silent. It felt so strange to be on the receiving end of behaviors she'd only witnessed from afar. Witches preached love and protection of every fellow witch. The young ones would fuss over the elders and vice versa. Mothers would coddle their children and prod them to eat a filling meal, regardless of age.

And her mother could hardly bear the sight of her scurrying in the corners like some unwanted creature.

"Peony will be up to something," Atiernan said finally. From his tone, Miranda suspected that returning to this topic was the last thing he wanted—but he desired to distract her from her thoughts far more. Why such concern?

Watching him, she couldn't discern anything obvious from his stern expression. Crossing his arms, he stood and leaned against the wall facing her.

"Liva was a cunning bitch, but Peony is clever *and* spiteful. Gods only know what she's up to."

"Are you afraid she'd betray you?"

Atiernan's eyes widened. "No. Never. But I wouldn't put it past her to devise some scheme to ensure we all wind up doing exactly whatever it is she has in mind."

"Something involving Marcus?"

It was a shot in the dark, but the subject seemed to strike its bullseye. Atiernan frowned, his gaze darkening with a hostility that made her shiver.

"The hybrid," he corrected. "I don't trust him, but if Peony thought the same, she would have had him exiled by now. She's up to something."

"You don't trust him," she was merely parroting the words he'd just said, yet she couldn't deny the sadness coloring her voice.

The warrior reacted to the emotion as well, his eyes narrowing. "You pity him."

"No… But I sympathize with him," she admitted. "Liva can be everything you've said and worse—that doesn't mean that Marcus is like her, or responsible for what she's done. But… That's not why you're afraid of him," she added, her eyes widening as the answer came to her from nowhere. It sounded so insane inside her head that she hesitated to voice it. Yet, something about this man seemed to demand everything from her, honesty being the least on the list. "You are afraid of what he became without you. You think you failed him."

"I should go keep an eye on that mage," Atiernan said, pulling away from the wall. "Get some rest."

"Wait." Miranda didn't move to follow him, but his steps faltered anyway, prompting her to add, "I know what you feel—"

"Do you?" He whipped around, his eyes ablaze.

"Yes," she rasped. "Because it is exactly how I wished my father would have felt about me. If Marcus really is your son, then you mourn the life he could have had with you. Years that you will never get back. You can never turn back time and protect him from her. That hurts you—"

"And you know pain?" Atiernan snarled.

But she did. She knew pain intimately, enough to recognize when someone else was trapped within the throes of it.

"Hating him protects you," she went on, her voice hoarse. "As long as you can make him the enemy, you don't have to risk letting him in. Letting him in—and risking betrayal— will break you in a way you know you will never heal from. That is what frightens you."

"And you know that for certain?" His voice was still in that lethal cadence, but his eyes alone reassured her enough to stand, still facing him.

"Yes."

"And how do you know that, witch?"

"Because… That is what I feel for you." Deep down, she realized she still wasn't in her right mind. She could always write this newfound honesty off as the aftereffects of being inside the sentinel's mind. Either way, the words resonated with a part of her she couldn't deny. And perhaps, it felt good to finally speak without scrutinizing every thought and misplaced emotion. "I feel like you could make me feel things I've never felt. But the thought terrifies me, and I don't know if I ever can. If I let you in… You can break me down in a way no one ever has. Not my mother. Not any other witch. No one."

"And that frightens you?"

She'd advanced toward him without realizing it, placing herself within reach so he could easily cup her chin against his palm. The contact made her gasp, her eyes fluttering shut. He felt so electric. So violently alive despite the many ways he should have felt repulsive to someone like her.

"Yes," she admitted, quivering at how intensely vulnerable that confession alone made her feel. "I am terrified of you, Atiernan. Though, I was always warned about you daemons. That you play mind games. That you deceive—"

"That we only care for fucking."

The way he said that single word made her sway, and an answering ache ripped through her abdomen, hot like hellfire.

"Yes," she whispered. "Exactly that."

"I will be honest with you, witch." He used his grip to draw her closer, letting his breath fan her cheeks. "I want far more than to fuck you. I want you wet and willing for me. I want you to moan my name. Damn, I crave things from you I have never desired from any woman. But I have been warned about the dangers of you witches."

With a thick thumb, he swatted a strand of hair from her face, stroking her skin.

"You weave your magic in every interaction. You wield your sexuality as a weapon, and you wreak havoc on those foolish enough to trust you. Which is why…"

"Why this can never be more than lust," Miranda finished for him. Her heart panged at how final those words sounded, though perhaps relief was the true cause? Finally, she could confess these strange emotions addling her senses—as well as admit that they would never go any further than temptation and desire.

Atiernan could never give her anything more than sex.

"It can't," he agreed—but he stood even closer.

With a heavy sense of dread, Miranda opened her eyes to find his gaze scorching hers in return. In a heartbeat, he closed the distance between them, crushing her body against the hardness of his chest.

She knew damn well what he intended to do as he lowered his mouth to hers.

But she didn't resist, meeting the kiss with hesitant, awkward motions. Perhaps another man would laugh, one with more skill who would be amused by her clumsiness.

Atiernan just ran his thumb along her jaw, guiding her into a rhythm that suited him better. Something slow. Careful. Careful…

She never knew kissing could be like this. More than a sloppy meeting of lips, but a dance of tongues. A game. War.

He showed her how to wield what little weapons she possessed, and then he dominated her easily, invading her lips with his tongue, threatening to devour her whole. Somehow, they wound up with her pressed against a bedpost, his body between her legs, his hands on her hips.

The kiss grew deeper. Harder, and their bodies joined in on the battle. His fingers gripped her thigh, drawing a gasp from her throat that he swallowed. In return, she tentatively flexed her hips into his touch, and he growled in pleasure, pressing in closer.

Soon, she realized that what felt like a very real weapon nudged her belly, so firm the shape took her breath away. There was no way in hell something so large could ever fit inside her.

As if reading her mind, Atiernan captured one of her hands and pressed it against his chest. At his silent urging, she traced the thick muscles, gradually letting the contact drift lower. Lower.

Then she felt the space at the front of his slacks, and her entire world shifted. She'd had him in her mouth before, sure, but somehow this felt more intimate—sliding her fingers against the thick cotton and brushing the hot, coiled flesh beneath.

He groaned, shamelessly bucking into her grip. She stroked him tentatively, using the clues he gave via gasps and shudders to know how hard. How fast. How long.

Suddenly, his mouth broke from hers to find her ear. "You keep this up, and..."

He trailed off, but her imagination could fill in the blanks. He'd do what he did the other night when those beautiful noises had ripped from his throat as he spilled his seed into her mouth.

The memory made her inhale, and her heart constrict. She wanted to experience that again, though this time…

She didn't want him in her mouth…

"Atiernan!" The high-pitched voice almost seemed comical, intruding on a moment like this. Until the doorknob began to turn, that is.

Only Atiernan was fast enough to shove her off and stand in front of her as Beth barged inside.

"Mother told me to tell you to…" She broke off, glancing from a panting Miranda to a stoic Atiernan. "Is everything okay?"

"Fine," Atiernan replied. "Your mother wants me?" He headed for the doorway. Only after he crossed the threshold did he pause. "It's the middle of the night? What could she possibly want at this hour?"

"It's six a.m., actually," Beth said softly.

Miranda blinked. Just how long had they spent talking? Hours? It felt like mere minutes.

"We'll get dressed and be down," Atiernan said. "Thank you, Beth."

"Okay… And Miranda, later, can you show me how to brew that one potion again? I keep burning it and—"

"Later, Beth," Atiernan insisted. "Give us some privacy. Please?"

"Yes, Atiernan." The girl blushed and darted into the hall.

But Miranda figured her cheeks were redder.

"Get dressed," Atiernan said. "I'll have a maid get the food. Meet me in the storeroom."

As he left, Miranda exhaled the breath she hadn't been aware of holding.

This man was going to be the death of her.

In one way or another.

⸻

When she finally staggered into Peony's storeroom, Miranda was inclined to compare the small space to a funeral. Not like the festive, witch festivals of mourning, but the dour ceremonies humans hosted, where laughing seemed a sin, and no one spoke too loudly out of fear of rousing the dead. Or, at least, that was what movies and television had led her to believe.

In this instance, a cauldron bubbled away in lieu of a body. Peony sat at the small table, casually sipping tea while Atiernan lurked behind her, and Marcus stood across the room by a shelf stocked with herbs, his arms crossed.

As she arrived, both men turned in her direction, though their reactions differed drastically.

"How are you feeling?" Marcus asked, his voice laced with genuine concern.

Atiernan, however, beckoned her to his side with a curt nod. While a part of her bristled at being commanded like a dog, she also sensed that to refuse would plunge the tension into a dangerous abyss.

In a fragile compromise, she sat at the table across from Peony and warily eyed the mage, who smiled in return.

"They've been like this all damn morning," she cheerfully relayed. "So alike they are, and yet so very different. It is like staring into a mirror, is it not?"

She cocked her head to gaze from Atiernan to Marcus and laughed.

"Oh dear, what shall we delicate females do amid such masculine energy?"

"That's enough, old woman," Atiernan scolded, his expression cold. "I take it from your gleeful mood that you didn't find the hybrid's story lacking?"

"Oh, his story is very interesting," Peony said around careful sips of her tea. "Very much so. That, however, isn't why I called you here. I have tasks for you." She gestured absently at both him and Miranda. "Who would like to accept their mission first?"

"I do have a pack to maintain," Atiernan remarked with a scoff. "I don't have time to run errands for you, woman. Besides, you never send another to do what you can for yourself."

"Exactly." Suddenly serious, Peony set her mug aside and threaded her slim fingers together. "These tasks are vital, but I cannot undertake them myself—or, trust me, I would."

"So then speak," Atiernan barked. "It isn't like you to dawdle."

"She isn't dawdling," Marcus pitched in. "She's giving me time to decide to speak. This task has to do with me."

"Ah, so you will tell him then." Peony beamed and nodded encouragingly in Marcus' direction. "Go on. It should come from you and not from me, as we discussed."

Odd coaching aside, Miranda had to admit that the air between the two seemed night and day to the quiet loathing Peony displayed before. Whatever they had discussed seemed to soften her toward Marcus in a way that might have made her jealous were she childish enough to admit as much.

"What are you on about?" Atiernan grumbled. "One of you, speak!"

"There is another son," Marcus said. "At least, one that I know of. Two years younger to the day. He lives in Hell."

"And he's awaiting your signal, no doubt," Atiernan growled, surging forward. "So that you both can fulfill your mother's wishes."

"Not quite," Marcus said without so much as flinching. "We've never met in person. I'm not sure if he knows who or what he really is."

"A likely story," Atiernan harrumphed. "One that I don't buy."

"Good," Peony said over him. "Because I do. You can play the role of the skeptical party in this scenario, and I will play the gullible old fool. Agreed?"

From his scoff, Atiernan did not agree in the slightest. "Woman, have you truly gone insane?"

"Bah!" Peony waved him off, but her expression was suddenly chilling. No longer was she treating this as a game. "I want you to listen to him. Can you do that? For me?"

"No bother," Marcus said. "As far as what we discussed is concerned, I can do it alone. Thankfully, I've gotten used to doing so the past twenty years or so."

"There is no need to be cruel," Peony said with the faintest hint of scolding in her voice. "You know that I am on your side."

Atiernan hissed a sound in between a snarl and a laugh. "On his side, Peony?"

"You will go with him," Peony said gently, though she wasn't focused on Atiernan. "Give him a chance. We can't afford to waste time over petty squabbles. You both will leave tonight—" She raised her voice, finally turning to Atiernan. "Find this other hybrid and see what he knows. This isn't a harmless request, Atiernan. Know that I wouldn't ask if I didn't consider it vital."

Miranda felt herself become enthralled, just watching how he processed those words. He hated being commanded like a child—she could see every bit of muscle twitch in defiance of it. Yet, something stronger kept him restrained, enough for him to grate out a single response.

"Fine, old woman. We go tonight."

"Excellent!" Once again, Peony was all smiles. "I suggest you two discuss the finer points of the plan. It will involve taking a portal to another part of Hell. Given that the location is in the same realm, it shouldn't be too difficult to rig the right spell. Go discuss. Marcus, you can be honest with him."

The younger man inclined his head in a curt nod.

"I think your study is private enough to serve well for this discussion, Atiernan. You should head there," Peony added, prompting the men to reluctantly leave the room.

Near the doorway, Atiernan paused. "You said you had two matters to discuss," he pointed out. "What about the other?"

The mage waved him off. "That is something that Miranda and I will sort out. Go. Go. We will all meet later, and by then, hopefully, we will have learned something."

"Peony…"

"Do not fight me on this," the mage insisted. "Time is of the essence."

With a sigh, Atiernan finally left, Marcus on his heels. Peony craned her neck to watch them go. Only when she seemed certain they were out of earshot did she finally sigh.

Instantly, the woman transformed, revealing her cheerful persona for what it had been—an act. Beneath, Peony seemed exhausted, and she drained the rest of her tea in a long, dramatic pull.

"We have much to speak of between you and me," she said once she'd swallowed. Facing Miranda, she leaned forward, her eyes wide behind their dirty lenses. "First, I need to ensure your trust. I know it is a big ask, but I hope that you are aware of the many nuances in this situation that make it vital that we know as much as we can. About every facet of Liva's potential motives."

"I understand," Miranda admitted. "So, what is it that Atiernan doesn't know?"

"That Liva appears to have born seven children in total," Peony said. "Six births, with one resulting in twins. A boy and a girl. Seven in total with a girl child in the middle. Surrounding her, three males and three females, each an embodiment of the six daemon races. The pattern seems to follow an old, nearly forgotten prophecy of a particularly alarming nature. Liva always did have a dramatic streak."

"What prophecy?" Miranda shuddered as the words left her mouth. Judging from Peony's dour expression, it wasn't a prediction of anything good.

"One that heralds the end of the world," she replied.

"That fits the descriptor of dramatic," Miranda said hoarsely.

"Exactly. Which is why we must confirm if that is her true aim and do so quickly."

"How?"

Peony's lips twitched into a shadow of her usual ripe grin. "Part of that entails what my plans for you are," she said. "Though, it isn't really my plan, is it? I suspect you've been of the same frame of mind since our last conversation and what was revealed."

"About my mother," Miranda surmised. "I need to go back. I need to talk to her. I need…"

Closure? No, something far more pathetic and trivial than that. She needed to finally look that woman in the eye and voice every grievance she'd harbored since those years of being a frightened child at the crone's whim. She had to know if her own mother had willingly played a role in Liva's scheme. Or if letting her child live had been her choice alone to make.

"There is much back in your coven that you would like to address, I suspect," Peony said. "Something I don't think Atiernan would agree to let you do alone."

Miranda raised an eyebrow. "Is that why you sent him on a wild goose chase for another hybrid?"

Again, Peony laughed. "Not wild. And I believe that 'goose' will provide much enlightenment regarding Liva's true aims, after all. But I thought it might be prudent to allow you to make your choice in peace without a giant blood warrior scowling over your shoulder."

"Thank you." Predictably, the absence of Atiernan did make it easier to think. Easier to see things clearly as they were.

And easier to acknowledge the clear danger that this plan presented.

"They never came for me," she pointed out. "Chances are, they don't intend to."

"And after days spent in the captivity of a daemon, they might not be willing to accept your sudden, miraculous escape either," Peony said shrewdly. "We must plan a precise ruse to see you brought back into the fold—"

"No ruse," Miranda said. "I think it might be better this way. I go back alone, and I face my mother on my terms. I am tired of living a charade."

Peony nodded. From her sly grin, Miranda suspected the mage might have been impressed. "You have every right to do so. And even then, they still might meet your return with violence. And we are not sure what exactly Liva knows or how much sway she still holds among that group."

"I've never heard her name mentioned before," Miranda said.

"But that might be for a good reason." Peony cast a wary glance at her empty mug. "Liva is smart. She would know well to conceal any role she might have held in her scheme. According to Marcus, we are not the only ones to catch on to the potential of the prophecy coming into play."

"And what is that?" Miranda asked. "What aren't you telling me?"

And why had her feelings toward Marcus changed so drastically, seemingly overnight?

"What did he tell you?"

For a second, Peony's mask slipped, revealing the real woman beneath. Someone exhausted beyond all reason, but determined to a fault.

"He told me something I will not repeat until I have confirmed it. Time is of the essence, Miranda. If I didn't think you had a vital role, I would saddle you with busy work fit to keep Atiernan distracted for another decade or so as I worked this out alone. But this is far too large a task to handle by myself. And for that reason... I must ask something of you that I know I have no right to. Something that I know may turn Atiernan against me once and for all. Losing him is a fate I have spent many centuries fearing. But in this case, I am willing to risk it."

"For what?" Miranda asked.

Suddenly, Peony reached across the table and grasped her hand, holding it tight.

"I want you to return to that coven alone," the mage said. "Face your mother and demand the answers to your birth, no matter the cost. This is something you must do on your own, and I ask... I ask that you do not tell Atiernan a thing."

Miranda mulled over the request in silence. Ironically, it should have been an obvious statement that inspired little shock—she would go home alone and face the other witches with her head held high. She would demand the answers of her birth and, armed as she was with blood magic, theoretically, no one could harm her.

Theoretically.

The truth seemed to be the very outcome Peony appeared to suspect, and wanted her to accept. She would return alone and open herself to torture and derision. Capture. Darkness. Perhaps death.

The coven, helmed by her mother, could see fit to tie her down and use her as a source of the arcane—and only the gods knew what else.

And she would endure all of that without even the slimmest possibility of rescue. Not that Atiernan would care enough to do so...

Lies, an inner voice in her skull whispered. The man would never let her go. She wasn't as naïve as he seemed to think— tender emotions weren't the source behind his newfound protective impulse toward her, either. Just possession. He was a predator with a bone, and she was the bleeding prey in his grasp.

Either way, the prospect was surprisingly terrifying. After twenty-eight years of facing horror and a living nightmare on her own...

She would be alone again.

"It is a monumental ask of you, I know," Peony insisted.

"You don't need to coddle me." Miranda gently pulled her hand away and settled it on her lap. "I never belonged here in the first place. I should have every right to go back alone."

"Without the possibility of rescue?" Peony prodded her glasses, nudging them higher on the bridge of her nose.

"As if a daemon lord doesn't have more important things to take care of apart from chasing after me."

"Nonsense." Peony laughed, but a deaf man could hear the scorn encased in the sound. "That man would follow you to the ends of the earth. I know it. You know it."

"So, is this your way of getting rid of the threat?" The thought hurt. She couldn't deny it. "Sending me back to the coven to die so that Atiernan will no longer have such a distraction?"

"Perhaps," Peony said with a tilt of her head. "I suppose, learning my true motive will require trust in more ways than one. Just know that I protect those I consider family. Not everyone Atiernan cares for is included under that umbrella. But those who care for him? I'd give my life to protect those few souls who show him loyalty. As long-lived as he has been, the man needs it."

"And what you sent him to do with Marcus? Is it really a wild goose chase?"

"Unfortunately, not," Peony said with a sigh. "That 'goose' will prove once and for all if my hunch is a hysterical fallacy or…"

"Or?"

"Or if we are in for a war far more deadly and harrowing than anything the sentinels present. Even the ancient race war between daemons and witches won't come close. We will need all allies, and all information at our disposal. We will need to fight for our very souls."

"That sounds far more important than a father-son bonding trip," Miranda croaked.

"Oh yes." For once, Peony's stare was serious to a painful degree. The façade of youth stripped away, revealing the ancient soul trapped within the body of a young woman. "We could be at the start of a battle for the very fate of our world, Miranda. And here I was, desperate for one day of peace to enjoy a nice cup of tea."

FIFTEEN

"The old woman is up to something," Atiernan voiced the observation the second he entered his study with the hybrid on his heels.

The dæmon lord in him wished he'd thought to alert his guards and fill the room with an entire battalion, weapons drawn. Not out of genuine fear, but merely to prove a point —he didn't trust this man further than he could throw him.

The warrior in him, however, scoffed at the thought of backup. He didn't need it and never had. Son of his or not, this creature would be dealt with the way he handled any other threat.

Without fear or hesitation.

Even if Miranda's words echoed ceaselessly in his brain.

The woman was beginning to display an insight into him that rivaled Peony's. Atiernan wasn't sure whether the prospect unnerved him, or...

Thrilled some twisted part of him that wanted to learn what else the witch could discover about him. His likes. Dislikes. Pleasures.

A low hum rumbled from his chest at the thought. Then he heard footsteps behind him and remembered where the hell he was.

"So, what is this grand plan you and Peony have come up with, huh?" he asked, spinning to face the man behind him. "You lure me to some secluded part of Hell, and a hoard of Liva's bastard children rip me apart?"

"No," Marcus replied. "I lure you to a part of Hell where I have to destroy the life of some innocent half-daemon who probably has no idea who or what he truly is. I have to inform him of Liva's cruelty and his own path of destruction. Assuming that the woman hasn't already made an introduction into his life similar to mine, that is. So, no. I'm afraid that your skills for violence won't be necessary on this trip. You stay back and let me do the talking. I would have gone alone if your mage didn't insist."

That sounded like Peony. Apparently, Atiernan wasn't the only one left in the dark as to the woman's true motives. Any other day, he would be content to sit back and let the mage take up the reins as she always had. This time, however...

Too much seemed to be at stake.

"Fine." He inclined his head to the desk and sat first, claiming the leather chair behind the structure. "Sit, and we can discuss this openly. What do you have in mind?"

Marcus remained standing, his arms crossed. "There is a section of Hell called Haedyn. Have you heard of it?"

"No," Atiernan admitted.

He'd lived in the realm since Hell's very founding, yet he hadn't freely explored the place in years. His fortress—and the duty of maintaining and guarding it—required enough diligence that left him little time to venture across the landscape.

"From Peony's cagey approach to this topic, I assume that the place isn't a meadow brimming with daisies with which to frolic in," he suspected.

"No. It is a lawless landscape little better than a mortal slum. It's where the lowest class of daemon gather, and it seems to be where my brother has made his home for the time being."

"Brother," Atiernan echoed, frowning at the word choice. "That suggests a familiarity with this creature more than you've alluded to, until now."

"No." Marcus inclined his head, his expression flat. "It means that I'm not so arrogant to assume that just because someone carries daemon blood—or witch—they are inherently evil and worthy of derision and scorn. Funnily enough, before we finally met, I always referred to you as Father."

Atiernan couldn't suppress a wince. "Your mother could also be cutting with her words when the mood struck her."

"Strange. I don't think my temper and inclination toward reckless actions came from Liva," Marcus countered.

For the umpteenth time, Atiernan mentally cursed Peony to Hell and back. Yet, he still had to admit that the old woman, with her many hunches, was never wrong. She wanted him to investigate this mystery, so by the gods, he would do so to the best of his limitations.

Even if his patience became strained to the breaking point.

"What do you know about this half-daemon?" he asked. "Does he have a name?"

Marcus inched closer and raised one hand. "His name is Logan Merris. He is twenty-six." With every attribute listed, Marcus extended another finger. "He is part-Shael—"

"Shael? That sounds below Liva's tastes."

Shaels were certainly known to be gifted in the realm of sexual prowess, so that was a plus. They were also base creatures prone to the same vices that tormented mortal humans. Drugs. Violence. Gambling. On second thought, they seemed creatures best suited to someone like Liva. While Marcus masqueraded as though he had some level of self-control, this so-called son of Liva's most likely embodied her worst impulses.

And would prove once and for all that, twisted upbringing or not, they were no different from the mother that bore them.

"When do we leave?"

"Tonight," Marcus said. "The mage said she needed time to brew the proper spells and potions."

"Such as?"

"A cloaking spell to make sure we aren't followed. A device to provide stealth, and a potion to compel truth telling."

"That sounds like Peony," Atiernan admitted. "But there is something else. I can see it in your eyes. Something you are just itching to tell me."

The man smiled, displaying teeth perfectly white and straight, devoid of the hallmark signature of a Raeth. "Lastly, she suggested I keep my knife on me at all times. She said you would gladly return it."

"The hell I will."

"I can't be parted from it, so if I don't have it, I don't leave."

"And why is that?"

Marcus scoffed. "After all this time, you think Liva would allow her children—whether you believe in our right to exist or not—to live freely, independent lives devoid of her influence? Oh, hell no. That knife is the one weapon capable of killing me. If I am parted from it, by a distance greater than, say, the length of this fortress of yours, for longer than a day, I will die. That weapon is my curse. So, I would very much appreciate it if you were to return it to me. Deal or no deal."

"Why tell me this?" Atiernan replied once he found the words to do so. "If that is the truth, you've just revealed your greatest weakness to a man who could use it against you."

"You can try," Marcus warned. "You need me alive to find the other son of Liva, something your mage friend has hinted she very much would like me to do. Should you stray from her plan, you can take it up with her."

"You say that as though the woman runs this fortress and not me."

Marcus raised an eyebrow. "Doesn't she?"

Fair point. Atiernan didn't know whether to be impressed or alarmed that the daemon had already picked up on as much. Still, another thing Peony had made very clear was that they wouldn't have long to squabble.

"Fine." He palmed the desk and sighed in defeat. "Tell me your plan, and we will discuss how best to implement it."

"There is nothing to discuss," Marcus retorted. "We go into Haedyn, find Logan, and see if he's willing to talk."

Atiernan allowed himself to smile, revealing his fangs, fully extended. "You are knowledgeable of our world. I will give you that much," he said. "But you still have much to learn. We do things as you suggested, and we'll be dead before nightfall."

"You can think of a better way?"

Atiernan hissed, sensing that this plan had been Peony's true aim all along. "We work together," he suggested. "You meet your brother, and I will cover you from behind. But I will carry your knife. Damn what the mage has said."

"Fair enough," Marcus conceded. "We'll do things your way, barring one condition."

"And what is that?"

"I talk to my brother alone."

SIXTEEN

Miranda shivered with exhaustion as she and Peony bottled the final potion created during their day-long brewing marathon. She couldn't remember the last time she'd worked for so many hours straight, composing so many detailed potions alongside another skilled brewer.

Perhaps never.

And yet...

A part of her hummed, exhilarated by the rigorous work. In the coven, witches regularly conspired together and studied old magical texts while brewing new potions. She never knew until now what it felt like to actually participate in such an event. Albeit, her current "coven" was composed of slightly more colorful creatures than the average witch.

"I don't think I'll care if I never stir another batch of potions again," Beth moaned from her position slumped against the largest cauldron, still bubbling away in the center of the room. "My arms feel like they're about to fall off."

"Change your mind about studying magic after all?" Peony barked from a spot near a shelf. Standing on tiptoe, the mage seemed determined to grab an item on the highest possible perch—though she shooed away anyone who attempted to help her reach it. "I hear the other children have taken to playing by the west fields. Ball base game or something like that. You could always join them—"

Suddenly, Beth perked up and began vigorously stirring the concoction under her purview. "N-No, this is fun," the daemon chirped. "So, so much fun! Though, Miranda looks like she could use a break."

At the suggestion, Peony spun around and fixed her gray eyes in Miranda's direction. "That she does. Bethaem, go sort the herbs out drying in the garden for a bit. I'll take over your stirring duties."

Beth frowned. "But mother—"

"Now," Peony warned. "Do well, and I will teach you how to make a potion to change your hair color. How does that sound?"

Beth grinned and shot to her feet. "Leaving!"

The moment the girl scurried out of view, Peony approached the table where Miranda was still bottling their various concoctions.

"Speak," the mage warned. "The real work has yet to begin, and already you look as though the executioner will come for you soon."

"It's nothing," Miranda said with a shrug. "I'm fine."

"Spill, or I'll have to use the same threat I use on Bethaem and force you to go play with the other children doing ball bases or whatever the hell they're up to. Have you changed your mind about returning to your coven?" The woman spoke with a sudden seriousness that betrayed the tension underlying this little brewing session.

Miranda shook her head. "No. It's just..." She sighed and let her shoulders slump as a mountain of concerns weighed on her conscience. "What if I really was meant to die at birth?"

"And what if I was really meant to be a fish?" Peony questioned. "The point is, I am not, and you are not dead, so what use is there in speculating?"

Miranda had to laugh at that, if only a little. Still, one fear lingered on her mind, growing more prevalent by the second.

"What if I was kept alive, not by a selfish mother but by Liva's decree all along? What if it is no coincidence that Atiernan chose to take me from the coven, around the same moment his son sought him out?"

"It seems our thoughts have trodden a similar path," Peony admitted. "I, too, have wondered if our meeting has, perhaps, been less divine and more deliberate. It would certainly answer more than a few mysteries. Such as, why

Atiernan seems so drawn to you, as well as the fact that a witch who happens to be a walking, talking vector for every arcane spellcaster smart enough to sense her true nature has lived as long as you have unscathed. But do you want to know something else that I have considered?"

"What?"

Peony approached the table and fingered a vial of silvery liquid. "Even the best, most skilled tactician can plan that adding the right amount of various ingredients, stirred for the right amount of time at the right temperature will produce a given result, such as a conjuring potion or a spell of protection. But there is something said brilliant mind *cannot* predict—" Her hand shot out, sending the freshly bottled potion clattering off the table. Instantly, the glass shattered, and a puddle of silver liquid pooled on the filthy stone floor below. "That a clumsy mage would accidentally knock over said perfect concoction. Albeit, should she scrape the mixture off the floor and bottle it anyway, it might retain some of its original properties. Or..."

She stuck her bare toe in the mixture and smeared it across the flagstones.

"Unforeseen substances might contaminate the mixture and either render it entirely useless or bestow upon it properties that the original creator never envisioned. One can only predict the outcome of a given situation, but there are always variables. Always elements of surprise. Remember that. Liva is intelligent enough to ensure that her future hybrid son would have a stream of fresh, newborn hybrid blood to awaken its daemon instincts and form a beast fit for her control. *Or*, fate itself could intervene, and a selfish witch might decide not to slaughter her so-called corrupted infant. It is upon those small variations of fate that life truly plays its hand, my dear. Don't dwell on what wasn't. Things as they are now, were perhaps how they were always meant to be."

"But that doesn't answer my question," Miranda countered, more troubled than before. "If I was meant to die twenty-eight years ago, what's to say that I can't still die today? What if that was Liva's plan all along? Bring Marcus to me so he can finish the task that failed to occur all those years ago?"

And if he ever tasted her blood—drained her dry—would the substance awaken his dormant Raeth instincts? Already, the man hinted that he struggled with aspects of his true nature. Who knew what could happen if he lost control?

Rather than seem alarmed by the possibility, Peony merely nodded. "I, too, have wondered that very thing. One fact, however, has tempered my fears a bit."

"What is that?"

"A far more dangerous flaw, I am afraid." For a long moment, Peony looked so grave that Miranda steeled herself for whatever horrific truth the woman might reveal next.

"Tell me."

"Well…" Suddenly, the mage threw her head back and cackled maniacally. "I know Liva. You and Marcus are so far from what the woman would consider a perfect creation that it is laughable. You both are too compassionate. Too thoughtful. Too stubborn. Too kind. You ache, and shame over things well beyond your control, and neither of you has yet to embrace the full potential of your various gifts. Liva may have plans for you both, that I don't deny. But you two alone are more than a bit of dirt or dust mixed into her perfect potion. You are, unfortunately, creations entirely of your own making. Now cheer up! Your pouting is making this place feel like a crypt. Though, ah... It seems your executioner has arrived after all."

At her words, Miranda turned to find a familiar figure dominating the doorway. One look at his gaze set her entire body alight. Whatever he and Marcus had been up to, unleashed something in the warrior.

A frustration that required an outlet. *Now.*

"I think it's time I stole the witch away from you, Peony," he said in a husky murmur that made Miranda's breath catch. "Whatever you're plotting, it can wait until later tonight."

"That it can." Peony clapped her hands and scuttled off into the dark reaches of her storeroom. "Bring her back by nightfall, Atiernan. That isn't a request."

"You'll have your way, woman," Atiernan called over her. "But first..." His voice lowered, rendering the tone out of Peony's earshot. "I shall have mine. Come."

He inclined his head, beckoning Miranda to follow.

Unsurprisingly, he led her upstairs—but his chamber wasn't their eventual destination.

"You will eat," he warned, near the mouth of a smaller, more modest dining room than the one she knew the rest of the daemons fed in. "This time, I requested simple, witchy fair for your delicate sensibilities."

Despite the threat, the food she found laden on the small table was far grander than anything she'd ever witnessed served in Hazel's Way.

After working all day hunched over a cauldron, she eagerly devoured her fill, sampling a variety of delicious dishes. As she ate the last of a fried cabbage cake, and licked her fingers clean of the residue, she noticed that her every move was being watched.

Right down to how her throat contorted around a hard swallow.

"You eat every meal as though you've never tasted anything decent before."

The observation was harmless enough, but she flinched at the anger concealed in his tone. She'd been lucky to even be provided with a warm meal by the coven, given her nature, and yet Atiernan reacted as though...

Well, the same way he had when she revealed how her mother would "encourage" her to perform blood magic. With abject horror and disgust.

"It wasn't all bad," she explained, driven to defend some aspect of coven life for reasons she couldn't fathom. "I was given free rein of the grounds to the extent that I could traverse the forests all I liked. I could harvest wild mushrooms, and practice magic in secret. I could drink fresh water from our streams and sample the sweet, ripened fruit at every harvest."

A genuine smile shaped her lips at the memory.

Until he added, "And you did it all alone."

She winced and set her fork aside. "I do not want your pity—"

"You don't have my pity," Atiernan countered. Miranda noticed that, so intent on watching her, he hadn't fixed a plate for himself. "You have my sympathy. Few have ever garnered it, so consider it a gift, not a burden."

"I don't want your sympathy either," she croaked. "I'm not some poor beaten little pet that must be shielded from reality."

"No. You are a woman who was hurt," he replied, his tone eerily level. "A woman who is still hurting. Acknowledging that pain doesn't diminish you any more than my sympathy does."

"Oh?" She exhaled in frustration. "What about your situation with Marcus? Does that deserve *my* pity?"

Suddenly, what little emotion lurked within his expression vanished. He was as cold and unfeeling as the legends claimed him to be. "No. It deserves your silence the way you seem to think your relationship to your coven does."

Tension fell with a choking intensity. Instantly, Miranda regretted rocking the boat by baiting him, but how to fix it? Strangely enough, she wasn't used to finding herself in situations that she wanted to fix, let alone was able to.

Still, she cleared her throat and tried.

"I'm… I'm sorry—"

"Don't be." Atiernan stood and turned for the door. "Finish your meal and then retire to your chamber. You should sleep."

"You spent the day with him?" she asked, assuming from his long absence that he had been as busy as she had. With Marcus? Or was the hybrid already regulated to his cell like an unwanted prisoner?

"And if I did?" Atiernan kept his back to her, his shoulders tense. "Would that require pity on your end?"

"No," she said softly. "Just curiosity. What is he like?"

"Like you."

She interpreted it as an insult at first—she doubted he would be as poetic as Peony was when it came to the similarities between her and the other hybrid.

When he faced her, however, she saw that her first impression had been far from the truth.

"He is stubborn," he said, his nostrils wrinkled. "Determined to have the last damn word in everything. He is self-righteous to a fault. Reckless in his planning…"

Growling in frustration, he began to pace.

"Were we back in the time of the great wars, I would have had to tie him to a post to keep him from fighting. Even I was never quite that damn obstinate. And his wit..." He shook his head, his eyes narrowed. "I think you've found your match in that arena, witch. His words cut far deeper than yours."

"I don't think that sounds like me at all," Miranda said cautiously.

"Oh?" Atiernan returned to the table and leaned across it, bracing his large hands inches from hers.

"It sounds like you," she said. "You must be the most obstinate, stubborn, and determined man I have ever met."

Did she mean the words as a backhanded sort of compliment? Perhaps. Rather than gloat in response, Atiernan inclined his head, mistrust glimmering in those fathomless eyes.

"Can you think of other ways we might be similar?"

Dangerous ground, a voice in her head whispered, and unease prompted her to gulp. Never in her life had she experienced jealousy cast in her direction—yet, she somehow knew that was exactly what this was. It was as if some primal, feral part of her reacted to the low baritone in his voice.

I belong to him. Or so he seemed to believe.

"I can think of one way in which you aren't," she said, raising her head to hold his gaze.

His fangs flashed beneath his upper lip. "And what way is that?"

"I don't know if Marcus is as unpredictable as you are." She swallowed hard, licking her lips to find traction to speak. Suddenly, breathing felt more difficult. She could barely suck in enough air. "Or as unsettling. Or confusing."

"Oh?" He leaned in, straining the table beneath his weight. "And in what way do I confuse you, witch?"

For the first time, it truly hit her—the fact that, if all went according to Peony's plan, she could wind up back in Hazel's Way before the night's end. Back in figurative hell, locked in a virtual cage. She might never see this man again or experience what he felt like. What he tasted like.

A life without joy and comfort, and the small pleasures he seemed to think required sympathy, hadn't fazed her. It still didn't.

But the thought of waking up without his presence, or his constant, unsettling gaze on her skin...

The prospect somehow felt unbearable. Impossible to face as stoically as she had every other hurdle she'd encountered until now.

"Witches aren't supposed to desire daemons," she hoarsely confessed. "We aren't supposed to want..."

"What?" His breath prickled her cheek, his gaze on her quivering mouth. "Say it."

She sucked in a steadying breath, fighting for a coherent reply amongst the mass of emotions rushing through her head. In the end, only three words sufficed.

"I want you."

She'd be damned if she knew why, or even how. Want alone seemed to convey far more than just his presence. His body. His kiss. His touch.

Gods above, she needed it all.

Suddenly, he lunged, snagging her wrist to wrench her from the table. She stumbled after him, finding herself racing through the hall in his wake, pulled after him like a log adrift in a fierce current.

When he shoved her into a bedroom, there wasn't even time to get her bearings. Was it her chamber or his? She wasn't sure.

Just that when he pressed her body against the wall, she eagerly arched into him. Gone was the doubt, shame, or the tiny voice in her head—suspiciously like her mother's—that warned she was a whore and every other horrible name under the sun.

She wanted Atiernan the Blood Warrior, and for the time being, nothing else mattered but that.

He captured her mouth, consuming her within a heart-stopping kiss—but one that lasted mere seconds. The next, he had her dress in his fists, bunched at the waist. Then he lifted the material over her head entirely and threw it aside.

Her heart lurched as those dark eyes raked down her body. She didn't know what to expect. *Not* for him to groan as if she were the most tempting thing he'd ever laid eyes upon.

"You are so damn beautiful," he grated. Thickened with lust, there was no denying the honesty in his voice. He believed that statement and more. "And you are mine, witch. Body and soul."

He was on his knees before Miranda could even process the words, using his tongue to breach her without warning.

She yelped, arching her hips against the unyielding wall behind her. He took his time, raking a pulsating fire to life with his tongue and teeth before using his fingers to make her ready for whatever he planned next.

A remaining bit of fear weighed on her mind, but when he finally stood and stripped his slacks, she no longer felt hindered by the emotion.

The man was too damn beautiful. Too damn powerful. Too confident.

He seemed to think he would have no trouble fitting all his throbbing length within her, and Miranda couldn't find the breath to argue. Instead, she gripped his shoulders, letting her nails bite into the golden flesh beneath.

It was a silent plea he seemed to understand, equally fluent in the language of fear and pain.

"I won't hurt you, witch," he swore, rearing back to hold her gaze. His eyes were alight with an intensity that shook her to the very core. For the first time in her life, she truly believed those words without an ounce of doubt.

More so when he grasped one of her hands in his and guided it down to his waiting shaft. Felt up close, the man didn't cease to thrill and intimidate. He felt massive, yet his skin was so damn soft, wrapped around rock-hard arousal solely for her.

"You set the pace," Atiernan continued, nudging her ear with his lips. "Wield me as you will, witch—not many can say they had a daemon at their disposal."

He chuckled—a sound that ended in a groan as she arched her hips and stroked downward in the same hesitant motion.

Pressing against her mound, the man felt like sin. No, like Hell, searing hot and liable to burn her alive if she wasn't careful. Still, she couldn't deny the hungry, shameful part of her that fully craved this destruction.

"I want all of you, daemon," she managed to croak out. "I don't want your gentleness. I want your—"

Before she knew it, he had her flat on the bed, his weight on top. Then he bucked his hips and she lost all train of thought. Her first coherent revelation was that he'd upheld his promise and more—this didn't hurt her. Even as he sank inside her, inch by precious inch, *pain* wasn't how she'd characterize the feeling.

Just fullness.

Awareness.

Awakening.

She felt as dizzy and breathless as she had the very first day she ever composed an honest potion by herself.

As if one small glimmer of hope had appeared amid the dark chaos of her life. That light had been enough to illuminate a path that still guided her to this day.

In that moment, she became a real witch.

And with Atiernan inside of her, she felt like a woman.

"Tell me," he breathed against the crook of her shoulder, his eyes heavy lidded, blazing like embers. "Tell me when you're ready—"

"Move." The plea came from some deep primal part of her that couldn't bear his fullness alone. It needed friction. Movement. The rough rasp of his flesh over hers as he drew her nearer, rocking in and out of her body with a steady, searing rhythm that set her on fire.

Her back arched as her knees locked around his waist, surrendering her body entirely to his possession.

If she knew corruption could feel so good, she would have left Hazel's Way years ago—a thought that terrified her almost as much as the pleasure building with every thrust did. Soon, she found herself writhing, chasing some insurmountable peak.

It was much like the feeling she'd experienced when he used his mouth on her but stronger. Every tendril of arousal seemed to coil in her belly, making her pant. Groan. Dig her nails into his shoulders even harder than before.

And as if aware of her desperation for that elusive sensation, he slowed, his mouth at her ear once more. "No one will ever hurt you on my watch, witch," he told her. "No one. This is all I will ever give you. This—"

He surged into her with a ferocity that broke the dam inside her and released a torrent of emotion in response. It felt too much. Too damn powerful a feeling to be sowed by just one man.

A pleasure unlike any other. At least until his lips found her throat, nudging a quivering artery. She could tell his aim wasn't to bite, merely to silence a groan against her skin, but even that small act was enough to remind her of the delicious sting of his fangs. The memory consumed her, so much so that she leaned down and brushed her lips against his shoulder in return.

The sound he made…

Her belly quivered, and her throat went dry. Perhaps, the fact that he was inside her—so large and undeniable—squeezed any remaining doubt or fear from her mind. All she knew was an ache she couldn't deny as she pressed her cheek to him in time with his next thrust. Voice rasping, she croaked, "Drink… Please."

He went still, and she could sense a range of emotions he didn't bother to hide—alarm, confusion, unyielding desire…

"Are you sure?" he replied, mouth still at her throat.

She didn't bother to nod or reply verbally. Instead, she tilted her head, offering herself to him fully.

And he didn't hesitate to bite.

And take.

SEVENTEEN

Damn Peony.

Damn her timeline and damn her obscure, unclear rules.

For the first time in centuries, Atiernan felt tempted to deny the mage her way and relish his own selfish pleasure.

Then he remembered that Peony alone knew his weaknesses better than anyone.

Miranda, however, seemed determined to come close to that same, unwavering knowledge of him. She kissed a path across his chest, slowly in a way that warned she was making a note of every patch of flesh glistening beneath his tattoos. Every twitching muscle. Every unconscious beacon of pleasure he gave off whenever she neared a sensitive spot or touched him in a way he liked.

This woman was going to be the death of him—but hell, he'd lived more than his fair share of lifetimes anyway. If this was Hell, he had spent a thousand years outrunning a pleasure unlike any he'd ever known.

And a moment, he would have to cut ruthlessly short.

"It's nightfall," he remarked, sounding like a man about to honor his own death sentence. "We should get back to Peony before the old mage comes looking for us."

He wouldn't put it past her, in fact, to barge into this very room and drag them naked into her domain merely to prove a point.

"We can hop to do her bidding now and return by morning," he added, and his lips quirked at the thought. What a sweet morning it was shaping up to be.

Miranda stilled, her lips pressed dangerously close to his left nipple.

"I suppose she'll come to find us if we don't," she said, betraying a familiarity with Peony's personality already.

"Right."

He sat up first, groaning at the absence of her heat. A million useless adjectives marched across his mind in a futile bid to describe this encounter. In the end, he settled on one.

The time he'd spent with Miranda had been *hers*—incomparable to any other woman who may have graced his bed in the past. It wouldn't even suffice to list the differences.

Instead, he watched her, marveling at how the moonlight played off that supple body. How her breasts swayed with every movement and how she kept her legs together as if aware of his seed, still inside her.

"I don't think she'd mind if you took time to bathe," he said. Before the witch could argue, he had her in his arms and entered the bathroom adjoining his chamber.

Peony would indeed mind, but he couldn't find the time to care as he bathed Miranda and made note of every inch of her skin. As the water drained from the basin, he made a silent promise to keep her here far longer next time.

Right in his bed, for multiple lovemaking sessions before he'd let her walk again.

"You're plotting something," she murmured, her eyes on his face. "What?"

He held his tongue. Let the witch think their relationship was merely transactional. Tomorrow he would prove that he intended to keep her here far longer than their bargain . But how to convince her?

Perhaps he could bargain some other sacred treasure, akin to the light wood tree? Or knowledge? Magic?

He would scour the ends of the earth to find something tempting enough to keep her here. To make her stay with him, damn the indecency of it.

When he finally had her clean, he dressed her in clothing a maid had fetched. Rather than one of Peony's dour dresses, this ensemble was a light pink sundress with short sleeves, speckled with slightly darker dots. Paired with her milky skin, she looked…

"Beautiful," he admitted out loud.

Which made her cheeks redden, and her haughty chin pierce the air.

"We should get back," she suggested.

With a sigh, Atiernan relented, but when they finally reached the storeroom, Peony wasn't glowering at them from the doorway, hands on her hips.

Instead, they found her deeper within the labyrinth of shelves and assorted boxes, climbing a towering bookshelf while the hybrid male watched disapprovingly from nearby.

"Peony? Are you aiming to find a way to defeat Liva or incapacitate yourself before we even know what the woman is up to?" Atiernan called.

"Oh bah!" Peony spat back, though only her slim leg was visible from over the shelf. "I know that it's somewhere around here… Ah! You may help me down now, Marcus!"

Obediently, the hybrid caught her by the waist and lowered the mage to the floor.

In her hands, as though it were made of solid gold, Peony brandished a small, metal trinket that resembled a hairpin she might have bought for Beth once upon a time.

"You will use this to open a portal able to take you anywhere within Hell. It will also bring you back." She pressed the object into Marcus' hand. "Be warned that it won't be able to transfer either of you to the mortal realm.

To try might result in bodily injury or death, so I would advise against it."

"And what will you do?" Atiernan countered. "And the witch? Sit here twiddling your thumbs to await our return? That doesn't sound like you."

"Of course not," Peony sniped while smoothing her hands along the skirt of her stained gray dress. "Miranda and I will be busy undertaking a task of our own. Pay us no mind. We will both be waiting when you return."

Atiernan raised an eyebrow. "But you won't tell me what you're up to?" He glanced at Miranda, surprised to find that she suddenly had a great interest in inspecting the floor rather than meeting his gaze.

"Don't mind us," Peony snapped. "Now go. Here are the various potions you will need. Marcus can explain how to use them."

"And what will you two be up to?" Atiernan tried again. "Brewing more potions? You are never idle, Peony."

"I will tell you what I'll be doing," the mage snapped, hands on her hips. "I will be here waiting for you to accomplish your task and hopefully get some answers behind what your past lover has been up to these last thousand years."

Fair enough.

Atiernan grunted and stood back as Marcus accepted the vials and potions, packing them into a messenger bag presumably borrowed from Bethaem—judging from the pink flower pin on the strap.

"Seven hours," Peony explained once they were ready. "I want you back by sunrise, and not a moment later. Understood?"

Atiernan nodded. That deadline wasn't a suggestion, but Peony's redline. Should they delay even a minute later, he had no doubt the mage would come looking.

"We'll be back, though, should there be any unexpected surprises..." Atiernan spared a glance at the man beside him. "I may return with one less captive."

"Play nice—both of you," Peony scolded. "Now shoo!" The woman waved him off, but Atiernan couldn't resist one last glance at the witch beside her. During this exchange, she had been too quiet.

That wasn't like her. Something was off, and unease plagued him, making him linger. It was trivial to even think as much, but perhaps she regretted their tryst already? He attempted again to meet her gaze, but she avoided eye contact.

And Atiernan felt bold enough to reach for her, grabbing her wrist. "A word, witch?"

"I think not," Peony said, squeezing in between them, though Atiernan merely tightened his grip. That prickling of unease grew into full-blown suspicion. The women were up to something.

What weren't they telling him?

"A word," he said firmly. "Don't fight me on this, Peony. Any hint of your mind games, and I will rethink following this little plan entirely."

"Oh bah!" Peony rolled her eyes, but Atiernan knew her well enough to suspect that she was weighing the risks. Ultimately, whatever she feared he might discover wasn't so big a threat that she was willing to risk her entire endeavor to protect it.

Still, as she stood aside, her eyes bore into Miranda's. "A word, Atiernan," she warned, with her gaze on the witch. "No more."

He grunted, tugging the witch to another corner of the storeroom. From there, they were still in view of their audience, not that he gave a damn. This didn't feel like some trivial boyish fling with a maid or servant he might have had far too long in the past to truly remember. He only focused on her when he reached out, cupping Miranda's smooth cheek against his palm. What she felt.

And she was trembling with emotion. This was more than shame or guilt for sleeping with a daemon.

"You're afraid," he said, feeling that protective instinct within him rise up. "Why? What is the little wench planning?"

Family or not, he wouldn't allow Peony to harm her.

"It's nothing." She met his gaze squarely, and he almost believed her. She stood tall, her expression neutral. After only a few days of practice, she'd become a vastly better liar.

Not good enough to fool him, though.

Strangely, he sensed she didn't aim to deceive him out of some misplaced or selfish intent. She didn't want to alarm him, but she was afraid. Afraid to let him know as much.

"Something tells me that whatever Peony has in store for you involves far more than mixing potions," he murmured.

And suddenly, nothing else—not Liva, or her bastard children, or even his own need to save his people—seemed to matter. She was hurting in a way beyond the physical, and yet, he still felt driven to help. This woman was poison, maddening and insidious, able to affect him in ways no other woman ever had.

But when she forced a smile and braced a slim hand against his chest, he knew it took every ounce of pride she possessed to do so.

"I'll be fine. If you don't leave soon, Peony might actually light a fire under you to get you moving. Go. I'll be here when you return."

Another lie.

Atiernan felt his eyes narrow as the predator he was sensed the deception. Only one emotion was strong enough to hold him back. For once, it wasn't respect for Peony.

It was the look in the witch's eye. A brief, fleeting, fearful glance practically begging him to trust her. Believe this little lie, or she might be pushed to some internal breaking point.

"We will talk when I return," he said, pulling away.

Marcus and the mage still watched from the mouth of the storeroom, their expressions unreadable.

Not that Atiernan gave a damn what they thought either way.

Let them stare.

No matter what they discovered regarding Liva and her schemes, he had already made up his mind in the case of the second witch to enter his domain.

He would keep her here no matter the cost, whether she wanted to stay or not.

She was his woman, and when he returned, he would endeavor to ensure she knew that in every way imaginable.

THE SECOND he and Marcus stepped from the portal, Atiernan was painfully reminded that Peony had a sick sense of humor. He couldn't fault the mage, to an extent. Spending most of her days trapped in the manor as she did, who was he to judge her for getting her kicks any way she could?

Though he didn't exactly appreciate that this time, her entertainment came at the expense of him stepping from the safety of his fortress courtyard and into a bustling, boisterous brothel, complete with women and men alike displaying their wares in thin garments made of silk.

Rather than the man beside him, Sanna would have probably made for a better companion in this instance. The sultry mortal would have felt right at home.

Though, the race of these creatures was far from human.

"Shaels," Marcus remarked from under his breath. He adjusted the bag slung over his shoulder as if aware of the possibility that it might be stolen at any moment. Shaels were nothing if not predictable in their greed. "We must be close, but this isn't the setting I envisioned for my family reunion. Let's go."

Atiernan was of the same mind. Together, they pushed through the sensual crowd and found their way from the brothel onto a street that looked like something from a mortal's nightmare. Safely tucked away in his own corner of the realm as he was, Atiernan sometimes forgot that his fortress had been specifically crafted to resemble the mortal world in more ways than one. The reality was that Hell had many facets. Unlike his haven in the north, this one sported a blood-red sky and a towering city composed entirely of glistening black stone.

In lieu of burning hellfire, however, was an overwhelming atmosphere of debauchery and lust.

"Haedyn," he surmised, judging from the fact that almost every person on the wide street appeared to be a beautiful, sensual, lustful Shael.

"We shouldn't linger unless you want to get solicited at every turn," Marcus suggested, leading the way. "We should find a pub. Somewhere secluded."

"And just how do you plan on finding this brother of yours?" Atiernan asked, scanning the nearby daemons. At a glance, he didn't spot anyone resembling Liva, at least. "Especially within Peony's timeframe. I'm guessing you know where to find him?"

"Something like that," Marcus replied while adjusting the bag slung over his shoulder. "I already made contact with him well before I sought you out. We even planned to meet."

What a surprise. Atiernan hissed through his teeth and fought to keep his composure. Even if the bastard planned to set him up, he held the creature's knife, tucked securely in the pocket of his slacks. "Is this your way of telling me that you've led me into a trap?"

"Of course not." Marcus scoffed. "This is my way of telling you that you might be walking into an ambush set by one angry Shael. I was supposed to meet him days ago in neutral territory at a specific time. That spell cost me a lot of damn money and was rigged only to Haedyn—meaning I couldn't even use it to breach your corner of the realm. Then a crazed witch used blood magic to teleport onto my doorstep right before the noontime rush. Suffice it to say that my schedule changed, and I couldn't exactly inform Logan."

"She didn't tell me where you live," Atiernan admitted.

When spoken out loud, the words could be interpreted as a threat. Predictably, Marcus stiffened.

"Not that I would ever tell you."

"That isn't what I meant." He sighed, fishing for the right words. Instead, he parroted two. "Noontime rush?"

Living in isolation for the past few centuries had rendered his knowledge of most mortal slang obsolete. In fact, it was Bethaem who had introduced him to many modern euphemisms. One small benefit of keeping around a young hybrid with a father determined to have her educated on the mortal realm.

For a moment, he was sure the hybrid beside him wouldn't answer. He kept his posture tense, his eyes fixed in front of him. Much like a soldier, focused only on the task at hand, unwilling to be distracted by anything else.

Atiernan figured he must have looked the same way once. Though instead of a backpack on his shoulder, he'd carried Conar's body, through miles of wilderness and enemy territory, never stopping even to rest. Not until he returned his brother to the woman they both called mother.

"I run a pub," Marcus said finally.

"Ah." Atiernan tried to suppress his shock as they wandered down a busy street he suspected was parallel to one they might find in any mortal city. Some of the daemons sported modern clothing in between others wearing more daemon-style garb. Large, flashy cars filled the roads—a marvel he could thank Bethaem for introducing him to. Still, nothing drove home the amount of time passing like hearing his son allude to a profession beyond that of a soldier.

"That's... Not what I expected," he admitted.

"You didn't expect your hybrid son, born of an evil witch and hidden inside a tree for a few centuries, to be a working man?"

"To be honest? No." There wasn't disapproval in his voice, however. Liva had no time for menial tasks, or running anything that required hands-on work. She preferred to perch herself on the lap of someone who did, whispering her whims into their ear.

Years ago, when he had been a simple Raeth under the rule of witches, his aims for his life—and any future children—had been simple. He'd dreamt of owning a farm, with plenty of land to pass down to several generations. He would have made offerings to their various gods, hoping for a son who would be strong enough to carry such a legacy.

A simple life, free from bloodshed and war.

Years later, he was no longer that hopeful man, his dreams were in ruins, and he had since learned that their old gods were dead. Monsters like Liva dictated the whims of fate in the absence of any divine beings. The only way to survive the onslaught was to ignore their chaotic rule.

Or, of course, hide in the mountains of a forgotten realm and strive to find some semblance of peace there.

Did he regret that path? No. At the same time, he couldn't help but wonder how differently his life would have turned out had he remained a simple Raeth living in simpler times.

For one, his old village had fewer people prone to ramming into strangers.

"Watch it," a man snarled while shoving past Atiernan.

He only got a glimpse of the figure before they faded into the crowd—blond, with piercing blue eyes.

"Let's hope your brother has more manners than the average Shael," he grumbled, not that his supposed son seemed to notice the disruption.

"This's it." Marcus inclined his head toward a building up ahead, and Atiernan tensed, all thoughts of rudeness forgotten.

Though it sported "pub" in its name, he had an inkling that his son's establishment—in the mortal realm—had a slightly more welcoming visage.

As isolated as he was, he suspected mortals wouldn't approve of a walking advertisement consisting of beautiful, naked Shael women performing a mere sample of the favors one might find inside.

When they entered the building itself, he quickly found that the brothel had higher standards in regard to its patrons. Boisterous Shaels threw empty glasses onto the floor, and raucous music blasted through unseen speakers. Half-naked men and women danced sensually on the wooden tables or along the long bar at the back of the room. All in all, what one could expect to find in a place like Haedyn.

"It seems your brother might take after Liva far more than you do," Atiernan grumbled.

"You might be surprised," Marcus countered. "Believe it or not, all children are not carbon copies of their parents. They tend to have some variation in their personality. Much like a living, breathing creature capable of independent thought might."

Atiernan grunted. Maybe he deserved that.

On the other hand, if this Logan preferred the slums of Hell to dwell in, how far removed was he from his mother's ambitions?

"You said there are more of you," he said, changing tack. "How many?"

Without replying, Marcus shouldered his way to the bar, where a hulking beast of a man appeared to be the bartender. After a quick exchange, Marcus retreated with two mugs of brown liquor and led the way to a booth sandwiched in between two drunken groups of men. There, he sat down at one end, leaving Atiernan to claim the other.

After taking a cautious sip of his drink, Marcus shrugged. "Enough," he replied vaguely to Atiernan's last question. "And I am sure we aren't all like our parents. Like how I am not you or Liva. Thank goodness for that. I am Marcus Orandus, and I have my own damn personality. I don't take kindly to anyone accusing me of being anything I'm not."

Atiernan frowned. Though the hybrid didn't seem to realize it, those words sounded exactly like something he might have said once. A coincidence, nothing more.

"You said a witch raised you?" he asked, changing the subject to one detail he remembered from their conversation in Peony's storeroom. "It seems your upbringing might have fared better than Miranda's in that instance."

He ran his gaze along the man's mostly unmarked forearms.

"That woman didn't harm me, no," Marcus said, his gaze fixed in the distance. "She was the closest thing I had to a mother—apart from the woman Liva murdered, of course. She taught me what she could."

"She passed on?" Atiernan asked, reacting to the use of past tense.

Marcus shook his head. "No. But what I am... It's far too dangerous to involve her more than she already is. I won't have her life on my conscience."

"So, you left her."

Marcus took another sip of liquor and shrugged. "Family means more to me than petty blood ties. I want to find my siblings and see who—if any—might have been brought up the same way I have. To think for myself and let no one dictate who or what I am."

An admirable cause for any man. Even Atiernan could admit as much.

Though that wasn't where the similarities ended—both men seemed unable to carry on a conversation outside of vague threats and insults.

They sat in tense silence for several coarse, blaring songs played through unseen speakers. Suddenly, Marcus sat upright.

"There he is." He flicked his gaze toward the entrance of the pub and the figure who'd just walked in. "Logan."

Atiernan warily followed his gaze, steeling himself for what he might find.

And he saw Liva, advancing in his direction.

EIGHTEEN

Peony remained in the storeroom after Atiernan and Marcus departed. Miranda didn't know how to characterize the nervous energy fluttering through her veins with every step she took across the dust-covered floor. Anxiety? Fear? Relief?

At least now, she would finally get to return to her homeland on her own, albeit constrained, terms.

That had to be worth something, right?

She hadn't decided by the time she finally reached the mage and accepted the two objects the woman pressed into her hand.

"This is something to help smooth your entry into those sacred woods should those witches be too suspicious for their own good." The woman guided her fingers to encase the object before Miranda could see it clearly. Still, the firm, smooth surface in her grasp gave her a clue about its identity, and she felt something in her quiver with reverence. *Could it be…?*

"And this," Peony continued, guiding the other object into her opposite hand, "is the only way we know of to get you between realms in time. I am sorry. I know you aren't a fan of this method, but I'm afraid it's all we have."

Which explained the purpose of the large, ornate-looking knife Miranda found herself brandishing next.

"I will leave you to it," Peony said before heading to the doorway. "And Miranda? I don't underestimate the risk you are taking. I want you to know that… Thank you." Her voice contained the hint of a sentiment far beyond gratitude, however. Was this goodbye?

As she finally left, Miranda considered dropping the knife and refusing this plan outright. The labyrinthine room and the cluttered shelves within would provide her plenty of cover. If she stalled long enough, Atiernan and Marcus would return. Surely the daemon lord would aim to keep her here as he once threatened to?

But then, her future would be entirely at his whim, living like a coward too afraid to face her own reality.

No. She shook her head to clear it and squared her shoulders. No longer was she the scared little girl terrified of the dark, easily manipulated by fear. She would meet this challenge the way she should have from the start—with what little dignity she'd managed to scrounge up despite years of isolation and scorn.

No matter what anyone said, she was a Hazel witch, and it was time to return home.

Surprisingly, once she finally faced the only decision left to her, it was strangely easy to wield the blade and lower it to her wrist. The sharpened edge required only the slightest bit of pressure to cut. The first cut was shallow, barely drawing any blood.

The second went deeper, and she could feel the tell-tale prickling in her bones that heralded the magic at her disposal.

You are corrupted, an internal voice hissed. *A monster! Beast!*

Closing her eyes, she tried to follow Marcus' guidance and keep her thoughts focused and clear about what spell she intended the magic to fuel.

I am Miranda Lightwood, nothing more, nothing less. All I want is to leave. I want to go home...

In the end, as the pain took her breath away and as the world was ripped out from under her, she had no damn idea where she might end up.

TELEPORTING WAS much like tripping over the threshold of a room—though the room spanned parallel worlds as alike in as many ways as they were different. As she regained her balance in a familiar field, Miranda struggled to process the feeling coursing through her veins. It wasn't relief. Hell, she wasn't even grateful to be back in her sacred lands, where she'd lived her entire life.

Viewed from just beyond its borders, the forests surrounding Hazel's Way seemed hostile and wild—a vicious undergrowth amongst which lurked a coven of women who collectively had never shown her an ounce of mercy. Or grace.

Two things a group of daemons had given her unconditionally from the very start.

And yet, she didn't hate this place. No, she couldn't. This would always be her home, and a part of her would always mourn for the life she had never been allowed to live. Had things been different, she would have had the upbringing of any other acolyte, graciously accepted within the coven's social confines, and shown the ways of a true witch.

But now, she wasn't even sure who to attribute her cursed life to. Her mother? Or a woman who seemed to loom over everything she'd always known.

Even Atiernan had been touched by her—had known her intimately in a way Miranda knew she could never replicate. Perhaps he didn't want her to.

Atiernan. As an image of him filled her mind, she was finally able to definitively name the emotion ripping through her chest. Pain.

She would probably never see him again. Never feel his touch or endure his mocking taunts. Even if she managed to suffer her mother's scrutiny unscathed, the daemon lord wouldn't risk stealing her away a second time.

And she shouldn't want him to.

Moreso than learning the potential truth behind her heritage, the one knowledge she truly regretted learning was that of the world beyond the forest she'd always known. A world full of men who sought to ravish and devour. A realm of violence, mystery, and a potentially better life than any that might await her in Hazel's Way.

With every step she took beneath the towering oak trees, she ventured further away from that faint possibility. And, as a shadow appeared on the path in front of her, she knew without a doubt that any future beyond these borders was firmly out of reach.

"Mother," she rasped, taking in the old crone who stood shrouded in shadow. Despite the darkness obscuring the woman's shape, she would have recognized her anywhere. For years, she'd grown accustomed to that very silhouette, looming in the doorway of their cellar, demanding she relent to whatever her request was.

You ungrateful beast! Do as you are told...

A few weeks in Atiernan's domain made her realize how distorted her recollections had been, however. Viewed from afar, Agatha Lightwood wasn't a towering sorceress, withholding the love and affection she'd craved since childhood. She was just a woman, one painfully slender in comparison to the trees surrounding her.

As she drew nearer, Miranda noted that the crone wasn't alone. Most, if not all, of the coven lurked behind her, visible at various points through the trunks of the trees. None of them sighed in relief at her sudden reappearance. They merely watched in silence, as they always had.

Yet, something was different. She could smell it in the air—a thickened tension much like the suffocating silence before a storm.

"Stop there, daemon," a woman called from the collective. Her voice was cold and chilling—haunting the few nightmares Miranda had dreamt of home while in Atiernan's fortress. "Should you mean any harm, reveal so now or face death."

"I mean you no harm," Miranda replied, hating how her voice broke. This time of year was stifling, a chilling contrast to the neutral temperature of Atiernan's fortress. Even so, she trembled, aware that her hands shook. To steady them, she tightened her grip on the small token of hope she had left.

Would it even matter in the face of her unwelcome arrival? Who knew. Peony had displayed far more faith in her than she had in herself. Already she could feel burning tears threatening to fall, and she blinked, desperate to fight them back.

"I came here merely to return home. And bring this." She lifted her hand, revealing the object held against her palm. Ironically, the pale, oval seed looked so small and fragile—nothing like what its eventual form symbolized. "It is the seed of a light wood tree, meant to replace the one that rose before my birth."

The assorted witches gasped, and Miranda could clearly make out a few figures as they drew closer. Her arrival was a cause grave enough to be met with ceremonial garb, apparently. They stood, fully cloaked in the black robes of the highest order—all but one. That figure lurked nearly out of sight, but wore a blinding silver robe that caught what little light there was. Alarm ran down Miranda's spine. An outsider? Someone important enough that even the crone seemed to defer to her presence, standing slightly apart from the center of the ensemble.

No matter their identity, the figure's attendance warned that she hadn't surprised anyone by arriving seemingly out of the blue.

Judging from their clothing, they had been waiting for her —no doubt after sensing the presence of her magic in the vicinity.

But were they hostile? Most of the murmurs traded amongst the women seemed to be of genuine surprise. *A new light wood tree. Here?*

"Lies." Her mother stepped forward, letting the glow of moonlight illuminate her face completely. Her lips were contorted into a grimace, her gaze narrowed and cold. "Don't forget my sisters. The monster only seeks to bring us death and destruction."

Watching her sent an ache ripping through Miranda's chest. When viewed objectively, she'd always resembled the woman standing before her—no one could deny that. They had similar heart-shaped faces with round eyes and straight noses. Their eye color was the main feature in which they drastically differed.

Miranda's were a dark, earthy brown.

Agatha's were a piercing blue that always managed to slice her through to the bone.

"Look at how it stands," the crone snarled, gesturing toward Miranda's body. "No bruises. No eyes sunken and gaunt with hunger. It partook in the sustenance provided by daemons. For that alone, death is what awaits her. But I will be honest with you…"

She advanced, traversing the path toward Miranda with slow, sure steps that resonated through the clearing.

"I wanted to show you mercy. You, who was born from my womb like cancer, I could never heal. We have shown you hospitality despite your cursed conception, and this is how you repay us? By bringing a corruption forged by daemons in the likeness of our most sacred totem?"

Miranda said nothing. For so many years, she'd done the same. Listened. Endured. Never ventured a word in her own defense.

There never was any use.

Until now.

"No." That lone word sent a ripple through the gathered coven. One might think she'd burst into flames and cursed them all to Hell and back. Though, in a way, she had. For so long, she'd withstood their insults and scorn in silence, never offering a word in return.

Now she realized that doing so had only made it easier for them to see her as a creature not worthy of dwelling in their precious lands—much like a sentinel. With one word in rebellion, she'd proved their beliefs about her faulty.

She was no mindless beast upon which they could project their hate and scorn.

No more.

"I bring you a genuine seed of a light wood tree. Not out of fear or hate or even guilt." Her voice rang out more clearly with every word, resonating throughout the clearing on a silent wind. "I brought this here because I believe in what this coven stands for. Whether you welcome me into your fold, I know what I am. I am a Hazel witch, and I will never forsake that title. No one can ever take that from me."

"And yet you consort with daemons," her mother snarled, waving a hand dismissively. "No longer will we grant you mercy. Tonight, it seems your judgment is out of our hands —" She inclined her head to the unmoving figure behind her, and Miranda felt a tendril of unease pierce her fragile calm. Was the figure a high elder, someone ranked even above a crone? Before she could speculate, her mother raised a hand in command. "Seize her! The daemon must be questioned, and our lands must be fortified lest she brought more of the vermin with her."

They surged from all sides though none laid so much as a hand on her. Instead, tendrils of magic shot from every direction to incase her in gossamer-thin chains, no wider than a hair's width. And yet, strong enough to drag Miranda to her knees. She only had the sense of mind to tighten her grip on the light wood seed before it could fall.

"Bring her to the inner sanctum," her mother commanded. "There, she will face the judgment I spared her from at birth."

Miranda didn't resist, not that she could with any natural magic.

Still, she wouldn't deny the small part of her that stung with the realization that Peony's fears had once again been proven correct.

Unless she utilized blood magic, she would never leave these grounds again.

If she happened to live long enough to try.

NINETEEN

Atiernan looked across the crowded confines of a Shael bar, somewhere on the outskirts of Hell, and saw the face that had haunted his memories for too long to remember.

A delicate construction of high cheekbones and smooth skin, too perfect to ever mistake—or ever forget. Liva, the witch, in the flesh, long after he'd hoped her dead.

And yet...

One observation kept him from drawing his blade—the body attached to her head was definitely male.

"Logan Merris," Marcus remarked dryly from across the table. "As predicted, he doesn't look very happy to see me, several days late to our original meeting."

Atiernan blinked to refocus. On second appraisal, the man approaching their table—who, admittedly, didn't seem very happy at all—merely resembled Liva. For one, instead of an elegant gown or silks, he wore a white shirt and denim pants that Bethaem referred to as "jeans." His hair was the same unsettling golden hue as his mother's, but cut short to frame his jawline. His eyes, rather than the shade of ripened wheat, were a piercing green that seemed to betray his true heritage. Neither daemon nor witch, but something in between both races.

"You stood me up," he said, his voice surprisingly guttural as he approached their table, his arms crossed. "I don't tolerate that shit from anyone, *brother* or not, Marcus."

"But I think you still tolerate money, don't you?" Marcus inclined his head toward the bag on his shoulder, his expression cold. If Atiernan didn't know better, he'd assume the pack contained a small fortune—not assembled potions and novelty pins belonging to a half-daemon teenager.

"Have a seat, Logan. Late or not, you still showed up, which leads me to think that—the matter we need to discuss? It's still very much at the forefront of your mind."

Logan scoffed. The only thing seemingly on his mind was a sudden thirst that he felt the need to sate by stealing Atiernan's untouched mug and downing it in one gulp. "Not here," he said after wiping his mouth with the back of his hand. "I don't trust public spaces, be them in Hell or any other realm. Pubs tend to have too much alcohol and too many damn ears."

"Fine." Marcus stood and led the way onto the street. "We'll go somewhere quiet then."

"And who the hell is this?" Logan pivoted in Atiernan's direction, an eyebrow raised. "You run with daemon hunters? I know the look of them."

"A hunter?" Marcus scoffed at the mere idea. "Him? He's my father."

THEY DIDN'T GO FAR. A few blocks down a gnarled road, the town's boundaries ended, and the wilderness beyond began, stretching onward beneath a blood-red sky. There, Marcus picked a secluded alley and leaned against a wall made of black stone, his head cocked.

"This is just for show," he admitted, his dark eyes fixed on his brother. "I activated a potion that will ensure no one around can hear our conversation."

"So then talk," Logan snarled, crossing his arms. Atiernan didn't know what to make of the man. He seemed muscular enough, but even Marcus looked massive in comparison. Despite presumably arriving at this meeting of his own accord, he sported a knife in his pocket—one fairly large with a black handle that resembled the one Atiernan had on him now, taken from the hybrid beside him.

"What is this about? You looking for some fucked up family reunion? In that case, I suppose a bit of show and tell is in order, huh? The name is Logan. Twenty-one years ago, I was an urchin living on the streets of some Shael hellhole when a beautiful bitch—I mean witch—came from nowhere and told me I was her son. Liva, she said her name was. But I already knew that—" He tapped his forehead with a crooked finger. "It was like her name was fucking implanted in my head. If I held any delusions of family and shit at the ripe old age of five, the bitch quickly quashed those dreams."

"She left you," Marcus surmised.

Logan cackled. "Hell no. She stabbed me in the chest and gave me the knife as a present. Told me that from now on, I couldn't let it out of my sight."

"Because it alone can kill you," Marcus replied.

Logan smiled in a way that strengthened his resemblance to his mother. To the point that Atiernan had to remind himself the bitch wasn't here—at least not now. "But you didn't call me here to trade childhood horror stories," the daemon went on. "What the fuck do you really want? And you—" He cut his gaze toward Atiernan. "You fucked the bitch, and now what? Regret playing your role in the fucking apocalypse?"

"What are you talking about?" Atiernan replied.

Logan chuckled. "Damn. He doesn't even know the full story of what he donated his seed to help set in motion? Look, I'll take your fucking money, but if it's a happy family gathering you're into here, I don't do threesomes—"

"I've found her," Marcus said softly. "Believe me or not, but I wouldn't have come all the way to this bumfuck hellhole you've found yourself in without a damn good reason. You want proof this isn't a fucking game? I've found her."

"Where?" Logan's expression changed, revealing sudden interest. He scanned the road around them as if expecting a woman to appear. "Where is she? How did you—"

"You think I'd tell you that? I will die to protect her. From you. From Liva. From Hell itself."

"Who?" Atiernan asked, though neither man paid him any notice.

"I don't want to hurt her," Logan said through gritted teeth.

"Who?" Atiernan demanded. "Who the hell are you talking about?"

"Our sister," Marcus replied.

"Oh, don't be coy around your dear, old daddy, now," Logan interjected. "She isn't *just* our sister, now, is she? No. That girl is the harbinger of doom, destined to end the entire damn universe. Liva sure knew how to pick 'em, didn't she?"

TWENTY

Miranda was crouched over a circle of beaten earth that felt as cold as ice, her hands pinned before her, her head bowed. It was a position meant to render those held for judgment prostrate before the ashes of the light wood tree.

Fit for punishment.

Witches believed above all else that mortal laws and constraints were worthless in the face of nature's wrath. The gods alone could pass judgment upon those found to have broken their sacred laws.

The duty of a crone was to act as an impartial guide—a mere conduit for that which nature intended.

Pacing before her, Agatha Lightwood seemed as far from that version of justice as one could get. Viewed in the moonlight spilling into the sacred grove, she merely resembled the person Miranda was slowly realizing she'd been all along. A scheming, reckless, broken mortal, desperate to avoid facing her own sins.

Even now, she couldn't look upon her own daughter. She eyed the path at her feet instead, her sandals slapping against the stone with every step.

"You have disobeyed me time and time again. Time and time again, I take pity upon you. And this is what you bring to us?"

The figure of speech was mainly for show. The other coven members were gone, lurking somewhere beyond this space, enclosed by the oldest, most revered trees in their forest. Once, the light wood tree dwelled in the center, a sight to behold for all the witnesses. Now, only a circle of charred earth remained where nothing grew all these years later.

Miranda felt a twisted mixture of awe and shame as she craned her neck to eye her surroundings. Never had she been allowed this deep into the grove before. It was beautiful, even bathed in shadow and moonlight. A haven of nature—altered only by a curved stone pathway that enclosed the area—where one might believe only the most sacred acts could ever occur.

A plot of land meant to be her graveyard on the day of her birth.

"Look at me," her mother snarled, drawing her attention. "Do you have nothing to say?"

Miranda couldn't ignore the tendencies she'd spent her life honing. To bow her head and meekly accept her punishment. To cower, despair, and hate herself for not being born a full-blooded witch. How sinful she must have been in a past life to be cursed with an existence such as this?

Ironically, a daemon served as the lone voice against such destructive thinking. *You and Marcus,* he'd told her once. *You are who you are.*

But who was she really? A woman too terrified of her true nature that she had never really embraced it.

But no more.

"Why?" She looked up, straining the magical bonds keeping her contained within the sacred altar at the center of the path. "Why didn't you kill me when I was born? Why let me live?"

"Why?" The crone whirled to face her, her eyes wide. Crazed. "Your blood wasn't fit to bless our sacred soil. The mere sin of you drawing your first breath cursed our sacred tree and caused it to burn. What might your blood do in return—"

"Liar," Miranda croaked, but she didn't believe she'd truly spoken at first. Not until she heard her own voice echoing back to her in an endless loop. "Tell me why."

"How dare you?"

"I know about the witch," she said. Up until now, she hadn't been sure of Peony's theory, not really. It seemed too neat of a coincidence, cleverly roping her into the complex relationship between Atiernan, his past lover, and their son. Too neat.

No coincidence could be so convenient. Right?

Now, as she watched horror darken her mother's expression, the truth hit her with the force of a punch to the stomach.

"She gave you the idea didn't she," she croaked. "You thought she was an elder, perhaps. Someone so powerful that you trusted her implicitly. You thought she could grant you power of your own. She told you to seek out a daemon, so you did. You willingly offered yourself to my father, and then..."

"No!" With a cry, her mother fell to her knees, shaking her head. "You liar! You twisted creature from Hell. I should let them do what they want with you. Damn you!"

They? The phrasing made her think of the unknown witch in the silver robe. While absent now, had that woman been sent by the elders to enact their judgment against her? But what...

For now, that didn't matter. Just this, finally speaking the words she'd held trapped inside for twenty-eight years.

"I wanted to believe it at first," she croaked. "That maybe, somewhere in that hateful soul of yours, you might have had a fleeting moment of sympathy for the baby you created. The little girl you bore in your womb until term. Maybe, for a second at least, you felt some small shred of emotion toward me. If not love...then pity. That alone was why you didn't let me die. Tell me the truth."

"It was our bargain," Agatha rasped. Her confession startled Miranda more than anything else the woman could have done. For the first time, she noted signs of distress she'd never witnessed in the crone before. Her gaze was blank, staring into space, and she tore at her hair with frantic desperation that alluded to far more than Miranda's sudden return. What had taken place while she'd been gone?

"Her. The witch with golden eyes," Agatha continued. Her gaze began to dart among the trees as if she expected someone to lunge from them at any moment. "I kill the daemon spawn growing inside me, and my power would be restored, my faith renewed. But as I toiled in labor throughout your despicable birth, I came to one realization. Just one. Amongst this pain, nothing good could ever come. This child was a curse. A monster destined for death. But why give her the satisfaction? I birthed you. It should have been me if anyone benefited from your accursed blood. Me alone. And what have you caused me after all this time? Years of agony."

Miranda couldn't keep the tears at bay even if she tried. They fell wordlessly, but she had enough sense to recognize that they weren't born of pain or even hate. Just an agonized sense of relief. Finally, she could relinquish any ties she had to this woman. Finally, she could be free of that one last, tortuous bond.

Agatha Lightwood never loved her, but no longer would Miranda be tormented by hatred.

Or fear.

"I see you now for what you are, Mother," she rasped. "But, oddly enough, I don't feel ashamed of what I am. Of the culture, I still love beyond all else. I am a witch. I always will be a Hazel witch, whether you accept that. I no longer need your blessing to claim the heritage you always denied me. But I am not afraid of honoring the other part of me anymore. I am part daemon and I refuse to bear that truth in shame."

Agatha made a sound in disgust and spit on the path before her. "You traitorous witch—"

"You said they are in charge of my judgment," Miranda said over her, returning to that part of the conversation. It itched at her, refusing to leave her mind. They. They who. "Who?"

With that one question, the crone seemed to sink within herself. In the blink of an eye, she resembled a lost little girl rather than the confident, powerful witch who lorded over this coven for the past decade.

"They," she said weakly. "Forces far beyond you or I. Far beyond…" Suddenly, her expression contorted into a mask of abject hatred as her gaze met Miranda's again. "If you weren't so damn selfish. So worthless! I could—"

"And this... A scene nearly thirty years in the making. I must say that I am disappointed."

Miranda didn't recognize the lilting voice filling the clearing, nor the woman who appeared at the entrance to the sacred grounds, cloaked in silver, a hood drawn over her face. An elder? No. This woman seemed too regal to be restrained by the laws of any coven. She was too tall, her hair a burnished gold that spilled down her shoulders beneath the fall of her hood.

"Have I waited all these years for this? A letdown, perhaps. Though I must admit, that there is no more fitting punishment for your disobedience than to see your own creation, realized before your very eyes. All that you have spent decades fearing. Gaze upon your failure, witch. *This* is the price you pay for your hubris."

Though she spoke in the grand, haunting cadence of an experienced, coven crone, Miranda instinctively sensed that this woman was anything but. Or, in any case, she hadn't belonged to any recognized coven in centuries.

She carried herself with an ageless grace Miranda could only compare to one other creature—Atiernan, the daemon lord.

But this woman was no daemon…

As she approached, she threw back her hood to reveal a face so breathtaking in its beauty that Miranda literally held in what little air remained in her lungs, unable to draw in any more.

Some deep-seated, jealous part of her had always insisted that both Atiernan and Peony had exaggerated the beauty of his first love. No woman could command such power merely through her looks. They had sought to diminish their role in Liva's schemes by blaming her cunning and guile.

Looking at the woman before her, she realized what a fool she'd been. *Beauty* was the harmless meaning of the word. The politest term to describe the perfect arrangement of various facial features that could lend someone more than a mere ability to convince those around them.

True beauty was a terrible thing to witness. Terrifying. A creature so perfect could have only been crafted by the gods themselves, intended to oversee their bidding.

Or by Hell.

"I must admit, I expected more than this," the woman said, glancing over Miranda skeptically. Her eyes were a light brown that rivaled the color of the sun—and were just as painful to stare at head-on. Miranda winced, and she found herself watching the woman's pink lips instead.

"A witch rumored to bring Atiernan to his knees..." She laughed, the sound sinfully lovely. "The bastard always thought with his cock, but still. High standards were never his strong suit."

Step by step, she continued to advance to the heart of the clearing where Miranda waited, restrained. There, the woman crouched and used one of her slender hands to lift Miranda's chin.

"Ah!" She winced, caught off guard by the pain lancing down her spine. While her skin glowed as pink as a mortal's, the woman's touch was...ice. Excruciating. As if she possessed no heat at all—instead, her body had been designed to siphon warmth through touch. And through her soulless gaze.

"And yet, I will admit that I have been vain enough, at times, to pride myself on the fact that the cocky bastard only chose me," she said, her tone musical despite audible disgust coloring the notes. "He was the first and most loyal of my subjects. Now I see. He merely had a type. Ambitious witches are a dime a dozen, but our Atiernan prefers them to be corrupted beyond repair."

"Liva," Miranda croaked in response. As Peony insisted, it should have been impossible. No witch or mortal could live this long without harnessing the most dark and arcane of means.

At a glance, Liva didn't appear to be a conduit of twisted magic. She was clothed in light and gold like a living incarnation of a light wood tree or some other sacred deity.

Had she been wrong? No one so perfect could mean her harm...

"Ah... Well, this complicates things." The woman stood and ran the hand she'd touched Miranda with along her cloak as if to wipe off any residue. "I didn't believe he would tell you quite so much. What else has dear old Atiernan revealed about me?"

A tendril of alarm ran down Miranda's spine. *Atiernan.* The thought of him alone counteracted any charm the witch could cast. Suddenly, she remembered every word he'd spoken about this woman in painful clarity. "Nothing," she spat.

"Oh, my darling, you cannot lie to me." Liva began to circle the clearing, fingering the branches of the surrounding trees as she went.

At first, she merely seemed to be stroking the various plants. Upon closer inspection, any leaf or branch she touched withered and crumbled to dust.

"You see, this is *my* domain," she explained, her voice eerily neutral. Each word easily reached across the clearing, no matter her location. It was as if the air itself rushed to do her bidding. "Anything that grows here has grown of my blood. My power. Anyone born here is under my influence, even you. To deny me…"

Pain. Unlike anything Miranda had ever felt, it sucked the air from her lungs. She couldn't even scream. Couldn't think. Her vision blurred. She was dying…

Suddenly, the horrible pressure withdrew, and she panted, drenched in cold sweat. Only the magical binds held her upright.

"I am not as sloppy with my toys as Atiernan is," Liva said softly, lowering her hand to her side. "I have ensured that I will always control those within my grasp. No matter the distance, time, or place. I'm sure you've already witnessed my reach for yourself?"

Did she mean the sentinels? If so, Atiernan had every right to fear the growing invasion of the beasts. They were linked to Liva. Linked to him. Such a spell went beyond blood magic. Beyond anything Miranda could comprehend. If it were the truth, then—in a sense—she had been responsible for guiding the monsters to Atiernan's fortress, though she hadn't let one in.

Liva had used her as the anchor all along. Or at least partly.

"You have a spy among him," she croaked, feeling no need to elaborate.

"Oh?" Liva's lips parted into a dazzling smile so bright Miranda had to look at the ground instead. "I can see that you are rather clever for one with such unclean blood," the witch remarked, seeming genuinely surprised. "I can hear your little thoughts whirling away even from here. And to think—" She laughed and nodded toward Agatha.

Miranda had almost forgotten her mother's presence. The woman cowered on a stretch of path nearby, her hands hiding her face.

"This one believes you to be a foolish, frightful little girl so willing to do her bidding. And yet, she still could not bring herself to cause you harm. She lied to you, of course, about why she kept you alive."

Miranda winced, hating the potential explanations that came to mind.

"Not out of love, no," Liva explained before the thought could even take root. "Jealousy. Why should a dirty, scheming, worthless little baby have use to the likes of me? Why not her? Agatha of Lightwood, beholder of several loyal generations of good, abiding witches. Why you, Miranda? She didn't even want to give you that name."

With every word, Agatha seemed to cower as if Liva were physically ripping them from her head. And with every gleaned bit of knowledge, the ancient witch stood taller, her head held high.

"She needed to call you something," Liva went on. "So, she picked the name of the most despised witch she knew of. A woman rumored to have nearly destroyed your coven once… I thought it fitting. Can you guess? No. Then I will tell you who that woman was—me." She smiled again, but this time Miranda couldn't look away, even if she wanted to. "Ah yes. Miranda O'liva, daughter of Hazel. A rather ancient, clunky moniker I have since changed for the sake of speed. I am sure even Atiernan couldn't tell you that much, could he?"

Did the man even know? Miranda knew better than to speculate. She needed to remain focused. Though, in her gut, a part of her despaired at knowing the truth behind the one thing she'd thought her own.

Even her name had belonged to Liva first.

"Not that I care either way," Liva said with a shrug of her slender shoulders. "But do know this—Every breath you draw to extend your wretched life, every day you live, and every moment you huddle under the sun was stolen from *me*, witch. You lived not because of this crone's disobedience, but because I allowed you to, long after you served your usefulness. Unexpected chaos can always be harnessed, and my did I dream about the damage you could sow. A witch cursed with blood magic…"

Her eyes gleamed at the potential bloodshed—but Miranda sensed that, never in her wildest dreams, could she imagine the destruction the woman might have hoped she'd accomplish. Some things weren't worth speculating.

Suddenly, the woman frowned, and it was as if someone had snuffed out every ounce of light from the universe.

"But even those plans were foiled. In you, I have found the most pitiful, worthless excuse for a creature—and believe me, I have experienced many failures in my lifetime." She approached Miranda and cupped her cheek in a gentle caress that burned worse than hellfire. "Oh, my darling girl. Your saving grace is Atiernan's interest in you. Would you like to hear how you will finally right a wrong brewing over a thousand years?"

Miranda kept her mouth shut. It physically hurt to hold Liva's gaze for so long—as if every cell in her body seared beneath the intensity of magic this woman possessed. Still, she kept her head high, unable to do anything else.

Against her palm, she felt the smooth shape of the light wood seedling as if it aimed to impart some of its strength into her.

"No?" Liva pouted in a display of disappointment and withdrew her hand. "Then I will bestow upon you one small gift. I will tell you how to right the shame of your unholy birth, witch. I will end your miserable life, and use your blood to open a portal straight to the heart of Atiernan's little hovel. Then I will go there myself and do what I should have done so many years ago when that bastard dared to betray me. I will drain you slowly so you can hear their screams, of course. Maybe I will even let him lie with me one last time, right here, so you can watch. Then you can die peacefully, my little broken witch. You will have finally served a useful purpose to someone. No longer will you have to dwell in my shadow."

She knew the woman meant every word in excruciating detail. And worse.

She would kill Peony. Beth. Atiernan. Marcus. She would take pleasure in doing so. And her blood would provide the power necessary.

Peony must have suspected what would happen, and Miranda suddenly knew with painful clarity what she was meant to do. She would never return to Atiernan's fortress, nor would she let anyone use her blood as a basis with which to harm him.

For once, she would do what *she* wanted. Damn the coven, her mother, or any daemon heritage.

This loyalty went deeper than anything she felt toward this coven, because—for once in her life—she sensed it was reciprocal. Atiernan had given her some small semblance of peace, and for that, she would repay him anything.

And to avoid hurting him, she would *do* anything. Witches may shy from dark magic, but a Vaer daemon always honored their debts.

She cleared her mind as she bit down, slicing cleanly through her lower lip. The coppery droplets spilling onto her tongue weren't near enough blood to power the spell forming in her mind. Still, it sufficed to allow her to turn her own body into a weapon, pushing blood through every last orifice. All she could see, taste, and breathe was thick, warm, red.

At the same time, her body became heavy, making her painfully aware of every bone and bit of muscle—and an object that remained in her grasp even now. The light wood seed. A part of her despaired that she couldn't restore it here. And yet...

Maybe it was more fitting if it too was destroyed right along with her, forever freed from Liva's grasp.

"Oh, do attempt a spell to harm me," she heard Liva taunt around a mischievous cackle. "It has been so very long since I have felt the sting of your twisted brand of magic."

Miranda didn't even waste her breath to warn that this spell wasn't directed at Liva, Atiernan, or even her mother.

With her final ounce of strength, she summoned every destructive bit of magic she could and turned it only on herself.

But for once, she didn't utilize the vast magic washing through her on a task commanded out of greed, hate, or even fear.

She only felt something she'd never experienced. To name it definitively, she could only guess.

Love.

TWENTY-ONE

"It seems you and Peony haven't been entirely transparent about your motives," Atiernan remarked coldly, his eyes on his so-called son. "There is much more to this than a few random siblings you want to contact merely out of a familial sense of duty."

"You're wrong," Marcus replied, squaring his chin. His focus went beyond his father, warning that every word was meant only for his brother. "*This* is duty. And we owe a duty to her —" He turned to Logan, his tone cutting. "Whether you like it or not, we owe a duty to her. To ourselves. No one else."

"What?" Logan threw his head back and laughed. Atiernan had to admit that the reaction was nothing like the cold, icy response Liva might issue. If anything, Logan seemed… unsettled. "You want to band together and serve as her willing cohorts to help destroy the world? I don't give a fuck, frankly, about the rest of the universe, but I'm not in a fucking hurry to destroy it, either."

"No," Marcus said softly. "We protect her from anyone that would force a destiny on her she has no say in. We surround her as siblings should, and we make a choice. A choice that doesn't take into account Liva, our fathers, or anyone else. We alone control our destinies."

"Bullshit." Logan scoffed. "That sounds nice and all, but you don't fucking believe that."

"Don't I?" Marcus pointed to Atiernan, his teeth bared, eyes ablaze. "If I fashioned my life after the destiny he set for himself, I'd be a bloodthirsty monster. I would have killed countless souls, and taken pleasure in it, don't deny you did," he added before Atiernan could say a word. "If I were like Liva, I would lie and scheme, and deliver all of us to her on a silver platter. But I won't waste my breath detailing how I am different than either of those paths. I answer to no one but myself. Marcus."

"And I answer to no one but me," Logan growled, turning on his heel. "Logan. Nice meeting you, brother, but I think it's time we cut this short."

"Wait..." Marcus hissed through his teeth, his frustration evident. "I can't do this alone. I can't. I can't protect her by myself, and I can't carry this goddamn burden alone, either. I shouldn't have to. We need each other—"

"Frankly, brother, I don't need any fucking one," Logan replied, whirling back around.

"So, then what will you do?" Atiernan asked, surprising himself. Wading into a daemonic family feud hadn't exactly been on his list of tasks supplied by Peony. Still, he felt driven to try by an emotion he couldn't identify just yet. Perhaps grudging, grim solidarity for the man who claimed to be his son? If anyone knew what it was like to plead for allies against an insurmountable evil, he did.

"Will you hide?" he asked of Logan. "Spend your time in fucking Shael slums and pretend that your destiny hasn't set a path for you that you can't escape? Denying such a fate may be foolish." He looked at Marcus and found the hybrid staring back. If he didn't know any better, he might believe he saw reluctant respect in the man's eyes. "But so is running from it. Your boon is that you aren't alone, unlike others caught in Liva's schemes."

He thought of Miranda, living in torment, and felt something in his chest tighten. Whatever he thought of Marcus, there was no denying that the half-breed had boldly taken the reins of his own life in his hands. To what end? Who knew.

"The least you can do is hear each other out, even if you won't resist your fate in the end."

"That's very fucking poetic," Logan snarled. He rocked on his heels like a trapped animal and raked a hand through his wild hair. "Look, I'll..."

"I think you *both* sound foolish." The voice came from a figure standing paces away, unnoticed by them until that moment.

At a glance, Atiernan didn't recognize him. His face was obscured by a hood, his clothing plain and nondescript. Though, on second thought... He vaguely recognized the man's muscular frame and stiffened, reaching for his weapon. Damn. He should have known before—there was no such thing as coincidence. This figure was likely the very same man who'd run into him earlier.

"I thought you said no one could hear us?" Logan demanded, drawing his own knife from its sheath.

"No one who isn't adept at magic," Marcus replied. "Who are you?" he asked, raising his voice.

"Oh, I don't know a thing about magic," their visitor countered, advancing steadily. "But I do know about Liva."

Marcus raised an eyebrow. Atiernan recognized that look—he wasn't alarmed but curious. "You are the other one," he said. "The third son. *Her* twin. Jacelyn—"

"My name is Jace," the man replied, throwing his hood back to reveal a face similar in structure to Logan's, but his hair was longer and his eyes an icy blue. Still, no one could deny their resemblance. Dressed head to toe in black, he sported at least one visible weapon—yet another knife with an ebony hilt. Judging from his open stance, Atiernan suspected he had far more concealed. "I thought I'd do you the honor of turning down your invitation in person, but that was before I realized that you have no damn clue what you're doing—" Upper lip curled in disgust, he looked from Marcus to Logan. "Reaching out to us individually, drawing us together under one supposed cause. Have you ever stopped to think that you might be doing her dirty work? And that is if I give you the benefit of the doubt and assume that you aren't her agent willingly."

"You mean he could be in on it?" Logan asked, eyeing Marcus warily.

"I think he *is*." Jace inclined his head. "Anyone who preaches resistance of Liva might as well be branded a traitor. I think you protest too much, Marcus."

"No," Marcus said. He flexed his empty hands in and out of fists. Atiernan briefly considered restoring the man's knife to even out any potential fight. One fact stopped him—Marcus seemed to meet his gaze and shook his head once. Facing his brothers, he said, "I'm just smart enough to know one trait I possess that our mother doesn't. Something that will always give us the upper hand, because she will never be able to see through it. Not with any damn magic in the world."

"And what is that? Blood magic?" Jace asked. "In case you weren't paying attention, there are seven half-daemons, born of Liva herself. You don't know of the prophecy?"

"I know of it," Marcus said dismissively. "But while we all may be part daemon, we are not the same. Not in the slightest. Unlike her, I believe we are all capable of harnessing a power she can't even dream of."

"And what is that?" Logan asked. "Some kind of daemon magic superpower?"

"No. It's simple—I don't care what we are, and I actually give a damn about what happens to us. *I give a damn.* It's as simple as that. A woman who abandons her children and believes they will follow some twisted internal programming like toys in a game? No. I care only about the games I *choose* to play, and I give a damn about what happens to the world I've been forced to live in."

"So what?" Jace countered, though Atiernan noted that he'd re-sheathed his knife, his hands at his sides. "You're saying that to beat an evil, centuries in the making, we only need a little love?"

"No." Marcus bared his teeth in exasperation, but his expression overall remained calm. "I'm saying that, to outsmart Liva and take charge of our own lives, we need to embrace the fact that we *can* love. We're capable of it, all of us. For better or worse, we can feel pain, hate, fear, and love. Liva can't fathom the last one, and that sounds like a boon to me."

"So that is your grand plan?" Logan demanded. "We all form one big happy family and hold hands and shit and hope that love alone prevents the end of the fucking world? I don't know who exactly your father is, Marcus, but I'm assuming he's the king of the fucking fairies."

"Not quite," Atiernan interjected.

Initially, he felt of the same mind as the other two sons— coincidentally, both of whom resembled Liva far more than Marcus did. They were creatures born of sin, inherently evil, meant only to play a role in a scheme devised by a cunning, intelligent, and very cruel witch.

No amount of love could overcome such obstacles.

But then he thought of Miranda, driven by blind devotion to a coven that would rather slice her throat as a newborn than let her live with any shred of pride or honor. She alone shrugged off her fate, and it caused her untold pain and hardship.

Yet, she kept living. She kept stubbornly resisting the horrifying end meant for her since birth. She lived in simple defiance of anyone's wishes but her own.

And he had never met a stronger woman, save for perhaps Peony.

"I think no amount of encouragement or words from a brother will change your mind. If you want to submit to Liva's plans, you will. Perhaps you already have," Atiernan suspected. "But if you plan to live your life under your own terms, you will. No one would need to tell you what to do. You'll do it. Even if it seems futile or worthless. Even if you have to tread that path alone, you will."

And perhaps, though many years his junior, Marcus had already mastered one skill Atiernan had yet to grasp after over several thousand years of living.

Pure, stubborn defiance of fate.

"Well, in any case," Logan began. "I don't think... Who the hell is that?" He inclined his head toward the mouth of the alley, where yet another shadowed figure looked prime to make an appearance. Two of them. Only, they didn't seem to have inherited the slightly more gracile form of a hybrid.

No. The bastards looked *all* daemon.

"Another sibling?" Logan asked.

"I don't think so," Marcus replied, curling his hands into fists. "They don't look like anyone I'm expecting."

"Bounty hunters. It seems I was right to come here," Jace said, appearing unphased by the rude disruption. If anything, his lips quirked into a genuine grin. "Your spells may be decent enough, but you've been followed. Tracked by a very powerful curse. It seems that one of us has been marked with an arrest warrant."

Atiernan frowned. "How do you know?"

"Ah, damn it!" Logan hissed, his eyes narrowed. "Because the motherfucker is a daemon hunter. I knew I recognized your face. Fucking hell!"

"And if I wanted to take you in, I would have already," Jace snarled. "Logan Merris. The bounty on your head is impressive, especially for a lone Shael to rack up seemingly overnight. You must have pissed off one hell of a daemon lord. Either way, this reunion looks like it's going to be cut a bit short. I suggest you go."

"Are you sure?" Marcus had his head lowered, and his eyes seemed a shade darker. Atiernan recognized the defining trait of a Raeth peeking beneath his stoic façade—rarely could they turn down a fight. Their breed was meant for fighting. For war.

"You don't want this fight, trust me," Jace said, facing the approaching figures head-on. "Just this once, I'll save your ass, Merris, but I suggest you lay low. These bastards will find you eventually, and I don't particularly care enough to pay your bail."

"Shit." Logan backed away, still brandishing his knife.

"I'll send you a missive," Marcus said. "Both of you. If you change your mind, come find me in the mortal realm, and if you seem worthy of it… I'll take you to meet her."

"You make her sound so damn important," Logan hissed, already paces away.

Marcus shook his head. "No. I think she is the most vulnerable one of us all. The only one requiring protection. She isn't like us, abandoned at birth and forced to grow up alone. She doesn't know what she is. She doesn't even know we exist."

"Lucky for her," Logan snapped.

"Enough with the heartfelt invitations," Jace growled, drawing a blade from his hip.

The two daemons were closer—enough for Atiernan to make out the dangerous-looking sword one had slung over his shoulder.

Gods above. Atiernan hadn't seen such a blade since his days in the war.

"Now! Go!"

"Come on." Marcus gestured toward Atiernan, and together they retreated from the fray. When they finally returned to the courtyard, drenched in sweat, and rippling with adrenaline, Atiernan wasn't quite sure what he felt toward the man who claimed to be his son.

Though, perhaps for the first time since meeting him, it wasn't loathing or disgust.

Maybe, beneath it all, was some grudging amount of respect.

The man had grit, and he would need it.

TWENTY-TWO

"You did well, I hope?" Peony asked as they piled into her storeroom.

Already she and Beth had a kettle of steaming tea waiting, and Atiernan drained his mug in one deep pull. Through a dust-covered window, tendrils of sunlight fought against the perpetual gloom and shadows obscuring most of the room. It had to be mere minutes after dawn, far too early to be plotting over an impending apocalypse.

"As well as one could hope," Marcus replied, his expression dark with concentration. Atiernan couldn't tell exactly what he thought about meeting his brothers.

The man didn't touch his offered tea and stared into space. Only as Peony cleared Atiernan's mug away did he finally sit forward, his gaze alight with a new focus. "Where is Miranda?"

Atiernan bristled that he hadn't been the first to mention the witch's absence. Perhaps she was still off doing whatever menial task the mage had set for her?

Or, more selfishly, he wondered if she was lurking out of view in shame of what they'd done. He could still taste her on his tongue. Hear her moans echoing in his head. There was a time, when sex would slack his lust long enough for him to forget the woman who satisfied it.

Until her.

Miranda Lightwood dominated his thoughts in every sense of the word, and he stood, intending to scour the fortress down to its foundation to find her.

"Oh, Miranda?" Peony shrugged. "Well, I assume she's dead by now."

"What?" Atiernan went cold as his mind refused to process those words—especially the callous way Peony uttered them.

"Oh yes." The mage turned to face him, wiping her hands on her skirt. "Dead and gone like the vermin she was. I'm sure they've drained her dry already, and Liva is gleefully siphoning from such a rich well of dark magic."

"Peony, have you lost your mind?"

"Don't tell me you cared for the disgusting half witch. Such a creature should have been drowned at birth. Burned at the stake. You should have drained her dry yourself and—"

Her sudden intake of air was Atiernan's only warning that he'd surged toward her, hands reaching for her throat.

"Oh, but you *do* care," the mage said, holding his stare, her voice suddenly firm. "Good. Now help me save her life before it's too late."

⸻⸻⸻

ATIERNAN HAD WITNESSED Peony in the darkest depths of grief. He'd seen her at her happiest, holding her newborn daughter in her arms. He'd witnessed her in love with Bethaem's father, enough to risk her life to bring their child into the world.

But he was willing to go so far as to claim that never, not once, had he seen the mage this worried. She tutted nonstop as she raced into the dungeon, leaving Atiernan and Marcus to sprint just to keep up.

"Damn you, woman. Will you explain? What the hell is going on?"

"No time," Peony gasped back. "No time... Oh, poor Miranda. May her gods give her strength."

Because the witch was truly in danger. He could sense it. Peony's loathing toward her may have been an act, but her first words hadn't been a lie.

She is already dead.

"Tell me where she is. What is wrong?"

301

"She returned to her coven," Peony said, spinning to face him.

"What?" Atiernan heard his voice echo back to him, bellowed and coarse. They were somewhere underground. Near the dungeons? Not that their location mattered one damn bit. "What the hell was she thinking?"

"Hopefully, she is thinking of you," Peony said softly. "And hopefully, you truly care for her. Truly. That is the only way this will work."

"What?"

Peony sighed. "My one attempt at honest magic. Now help me lift this. Hurry!" She gestured to a stone slab before them.

With a start, Atiernan realized exactly where they were. The crypt. But why...

"Come on, Atiernan, I cannot do this alone," Peony snapped, though Marcus had already rushed to assist her. "If my plan worked, all will be well. If not, then we have but mere moments to clear this land for good. Either way, you standing there gaping like a fool will not help. By the gods, get over here and help me!"

Atiernan lurched into motion, gripping one end of the slab while Peony and Marcus steadied the other. Together, they heaved the piece aside, revealing the chamber beneath.

But Atiernan figured he would have never been prepared for what he found inside.

TWENTY-THREE

Miranda thought death would be silent, cold, and finite. An echo chamber from inside which all of her failures would resonate.

Instead, she just heard worried voices, and while she felt cold, it wasn't the endless sort of chill one might expect to suffer in the afterlife. Instead, this solitude was itchy and reeked of mildew. The darkness was suffocating, and the voices...

They were familiar.

"Hurry! Fall back. Give her some air."

Suddenly, warmth descended upon her from all sides. Tendrils of it smoothed the damp hair from her head and caressed her forehead. Fingers?

"Miranda? Can you hear me?"

"Atiernan," a voice warned. "Be careful. She's bleeding."

So much blood, she was drenched in it. Apparently, death hadn't found her yet, but she could feel it creeping closer like a specter, waiting to swallow her whole.

"Peony, do something!"

"It is alright," the mage replied. "Just let her breathe. Let us just hope that you are not overcome by bloodlust and cause her further harm in this weakened state. She will live, I am sure, but she will need days of rest. Marcus, if you could find Bethaem and set about brewing a pot of tea. Some healing salve, perhaps, and some fresh rags—"

"Of course!"

Footsteps echoed, racing away, but Miranda could barely focus her vision enough to even know where she was. Somewhere dark, though not quite.

Eyes like fire pierced the shadow, lighting her way back to the land of the living.

"Where... How?" she croaked.

"Pull her from that accursed place, will you, Atiernan! Set her down. Gently. Gently. Once she has recovered a bit more, we will move her to one of the empty chambers—"

"No," a deep voice declared. "We'll bring her to mine."

"Oh bah! Anywhere is better than a cold stone floor."

Suddenly, another set of eyes appeared beside the first—a wide, open gray distorted by round lenses.

"Oh, my girl," Peony murmured. "My poor, sweet girl. I actually didn't believe that plan would work, but you succeeded my best hopes—"

"You sent her there like a lamb to slaughter," Atiernan growled. "What the hell is wrong with you?"

"No," Peony insisted. "I made a gamble. A gamble with all our lives and safety on the line. You should just be grateful that it has paid off. For the time being, at least, no one will be able to harm us here. Thanks to Miranda. Oh, my precious girl—"

"What spell?" Atiernan demanded. "Answer me, woman!"

"Liva had a trap set, waiting to be sprung. So, I set one of my own," Peony replied coldly. "I know that cunning witch. I know she suspected that a witch born into a coven—even one that despised her—would be driven to return, if only for answers. Answers only a mother could give. Liva would have prided herself in being there, and I am sure she took great pleasure in believing she had a direct link to you. So, I did what any *real* mother would," Peony added. "I placed faith in the goodness of my child's soul and hoped that Miranda would not succumb to pain and fear. Oh, I know the sacrifice you were willing to make, my dear," the mage said, stroking Miranda's cheek. "One that I will never voice aloud, but believe that I understand how hard it was to make. Whether you decide to reveal it or not is your choice, but know that we can never repay such a gift."

"What are you talking about?" Atiernan interjected. "What happened?"

"I took a risk and attempted to craft my own spell," Peony went on, ignoring him. "One too powerful to rely on either witch or daemon magic. A craft long since lost to the ravages of time and overlooked in favor of greed. It was your friend Marcus, who suggested it. A protection spell simple in essence, but for it to work requires far more than blood."

"What?" Atiernan asked, though Miranda suspected she already knew the answer.

Somewhere, deep down, she might have always known the second she decided to return to Hazel's Way.

"Love," Peony said simply. "A damn powerful magic but almost impossible to harness. It must be real, that love. It must outlast everything else. All hate, pain, and shame. It must be genuine enough in the face of untold suffering and loss, and it alone can outwit death itself. I do not underestimate the sacrifice you were willing to make, Miranda. But know this—here you are safe, and you are loved. Your coven may have cast you out, but you will always have a place here, should you choose it."

She didn't understand the words. She was too exhausted to think. All she could do was go limp, relishing the feel of the body holding her close.

Internally, she felt something relax. Like a tense muscle that had been bearing a silent burden for the past twenty-eight years. Since her birth.

A heavy weight that was finally lifted after so very long.

It felt more freeing than any feeling she could ever remember experiencing.

It felt like freedom, but she wasn't the only one deserving such a gift. The thought spurred her to open her eyes, though even that bit of exertion pushed her depleted muscles to their limit.

So did speaking.

"The sentinel," she croaked, fighting for the strength just to get the words out.

"Damn the beast," Atiernan snarled. "You need rest—"

With difficulty, Miranda shook her head. "I think… I think I know how to help it."

"Just sleep. They should be the furthest thing from your mind now."

But they weren't. Liva had been confident in her plan for a reason. The threat wasn't over—not by a long shot.

"How?" another voice asked. Marcus, appearing with a handful of the materials Peony had requested.

"The tree," Miranda rasped. Even now, she could feel it in her grasp, somehow rescued amid the chaos of her ordeal back at Hazel's Way. One day, she would restore her coven's sacred ornament, but deep in her soul, she sensed it wouldn't be any time soon.

That didn't mean the gift had to be wasted before then.

"They need it more," she continued, picturing the decaying, corrupted abomination destroying their lands. "I can endow it with a spell of protection... That might be enough to stop the attacks. Otherwise… I think Liva is relying on them as a failsafe. She wants you dead—" Her gaze cut to Atiernan. "Needs you gone. I don't know why. But…helping the sentinels. That could stop her."

And keep Atiernan and his people safe for now—the least she could do in turn for what they'd seemingly done for her. Her brain was too strained to truly process the meaning of Peony's words, but she got the gist.

The mage had done a spell powerful enough to outlast even death.

She might as well make use of the life she'd managed to salvage.

"That's all good and well," Peony said sternly. "But now?" The mage brushed her hand along Miranda's forehead. That gentle encouragement seemed to be the cue her body needed to surrender to its exhaustion.

"Sleep," the mage encouraged as her vision went black. "Just sleep."

"Even if you stop touching me, I don't think I'll fade away," Miranda murmured, her eyes still closed.

The fingers stroking relentlessly through her hair didn't cease their gentle assault. They merely stilled for a heartbeat, long enough for their owner to say in response, "Even if you wanted to fade away, witch, I would use more than my hands to keep you here."

The promise resonated to her core, voiced in a heated baritone that made her wish she had enough strength in her limbs to reply.

"There will be plenty of time to demonstrate, later," Atiernan went on, as if aware of her thoughts. "Once you fully heal, I will take great pleasure in showing how I plan on keeping you here, no matter what fate demands."

Which brought to mind another pressing dilemma. Groaning, she shot upright, clutching her throbbing head with one hand. With the other, she grasped Atiernan's forearm.

"What's wrong?" His voice resonated with so much genuine concern her already pounding head felt liable to float away on the resulting wave of selfish pride—he cared for her.

But would he still if banishing her from his realm was the only way to save his people?

"Liva has an anchor here," she managed to rasp. "It isn't strong, but someone with a link to her tenuous enough to guide the sentinels here, among other horrors. If you don't stamp it out…"

"Stamp it out how?" the warrior demanded. "And can it wait until after you've been bathed and fed?" He gestured to her blood-caked sundress.

"No." Miranda met his gaze, and whatever he saw in her expression made him nod just once. "I see. And how do we find this anchor?"

Miranda looked down, eyeing the silken sheets tangled around their limbs. She still felt so weak. Using blood magic in this state might kill her—but would that fear stop her from doing whatever was necessary to flee this realm and minimize the risk to the man beside her and everyone under his roof?

No.

"Peony shouldn't have wasted such a powerful spell to bring me back," she said softly, feeling her eyes well with unshed tears. It seemed so damn…unfair. To finally find some shred of solace and people who didn't cringe at the very sight of her. Only to have no choice but to distance herself from them indefinitely.

"You think it's you." Abruptly, Atiernan withdrew his arm and leveled her with a look that stole her breath.

"Yes," she confessed. "And for the sake of everyone here, I need to leave. Now. I'm too weak to teleport on my own, but if Peony still has another—"

"You aren't going anywhere." The intensity in his tone made her heart skip a beat—as did his pigheaded refusal to understand the danger she presented.

"I stay, and Liva will always have a foothold here," she insisted. "Always. It will only be a matter of time before one of her attacks finds its mark."

"But—" The warrior grabbed her wrist before she could even think to move. "You're forgetting one thing—these attacks began long before you came here. Their escalation is why I sought out a witch in the first place. I don't think you could serve as the anchor for Liva's spells while living secluded in your forest, do you?"

He had a point.

"No," Miranda admitted. "But then who else? I don't think a full-blooded daemon could serve as the anchor. Unless you have another witch around here somewhere, then I don't see—"

"No, not a daemon," Atiernan said gravely. What exactly he thought? She couldn't tell. The next second, he hauled her into his arms and stormed into the bathroom to bathe her despite her insistence on the opposite.

Any argument, however, died in her throat as he settled into the tub behind her, leaving her no choice but to lean back against his chest. He washed her quickly, but still with the uncanny gentleness that made her feel like a porcelain doll. Or perhaps not an inanimate object, but a living being he cared for enough to treat with the utmost care.

She let herself be lulled into a false sense of security and nearly missed the moment he brought a finger to her lips and coaxed them to part—a finger, smeared with a suspiciously red substance.

"Atiernan—"

"A drop, or you'll be too weak to withstand what I have planned," he replied, his lips against her ear. "Humor me, witch."

With a sigh, she relented, ignoring the vicious craving his taste alone inspired. Somehow, she managed to keep herself from begging for more, and Atiernan finished his ministrations in silence.

Once she was dressed in one of Peony's borrowed gowns, he promptly carried her into the hallway. "There is one way to solve this," he began, his voice rumbling through his chest and into her very bones. "A crude method, admittedly, but one that will prove results, I am sure. You are half-right—you aren't the anchor, but someone else must be."

"No one else *can* be," Miranda countered. She strived to make her voice as firm and level as possible, not that a word seemed to penetrate the beautiful skull of the man tearing through the manor like a bat out of hell.

"The only way to keep those you care for safe is for me to—"

"Do you trust me?"

The question came as the daemon stopped short, startling a nearby group of women who rushed to avoid him.

"Do you?" His fiery eyes were fixed straight ahead, his expression stoic. She wasn't fooled. Whatever her answer may be, he agonized over it. A fact that puzzled her and a tiny bit of amusement went to war with her overwhelming dread.

"I do," she said. "But I don't think my trust matters much in this instance. It is you who needs to have faith in me—"

"I do," he said over her. Tightening his grip, he continued to carry her down the main staircase at a speed that made her teeth chatter. "Which is why I know in my gut that you are not the anchor. Now it is your turn to put your faith in me. Know that I would never hurt you. Never. But you hear me good and hear me now, witch—I'm not letting you go, either."

As he turned into the great hall, Miranda noted that he had enough tact to avoid adding a determinative word to that phrasing. One she could guess anyway.

I'm not letting you go ever.

There wasn't even time to marvel—or react with horror—at that assurance. A heartbeat later, she found herself propped onto a leather chair while Atiernan circled the massive chamber, shouting in a way fit to rouse the whole house. The words echoed, distorting them. Only when he turned to face her could Miranda discern exactly what he was saying.

"Everyone of maturity, gather here now. I call a tribunal."

TWENTY-FOUR

Tribunals were messy affairs. Despite his threat to the witch, Atiernan had never initiated one himself. It was an old, archaic way of doing things. Even though he was reclusive, he considered himself a fairly progressive leader in most cases.

Progressive enough to allow those within his domain a steady supply of whatever comforts they desired from the outside world—humans among them. Sure, he wouldn't deny that it had crossed his mind once or twice that such imports may be used for insidious means by any enemies who sought to harm him, Liva paramount among them.

He just didn't think the bitch would be clever enough to attack one weakness of his *she* herself had inflicted. A vow he'd made with only her betrayal in mind.

Miranda could have been the anchor, as she feared, but Atiernan could think of another fitting suspect. But would his hunch pay off?

That remained to be seen. The only alternative was one he could still sense forming in the witch's mind, even as she kept her face angled away from him. She'd use that corrupted magic of hers one final time and leave. She'd run back to the mortal realm—or worse, run right to the witches who sought to cause her only pain and isolation.

Not if he had any say in it.

Stone-faced, he stewed in the varying problems weighing on his mind as those in the manor rushed to heed his call. When Peony entered the room, she gave him a single glance, her eyebrow raised inquisitively. Atiernan got the sense the old woman already knew the topic of this impromptu meeting.

And if Peony herself hadn't advocated for Miranda's removal from the start, he suspected that she had reached the same conclusion he had. Why keep the true culprit to herself? He could only wonder.

For now, it was his turn to take the reins of the title he rarely acknowledged.

That of a daemon lord.

"Someone among us is a spy for an evil only the most long-lived here will remember," he began, satisfied as a majority of his people crowded into the great room. "A cunning, viper of a woman who seeks to bring us all harm—"

"The witch!" someone cried out, among a few murmurs of agreement. Many turned to Miranda, who watched him from behind the desk he usually claimed for himself, her eyes wide with confusion.

Despite the current circumstances, the look excited him. How many other ways could he catch the woman off guard? Testing said theory would have to wait, however.

"Yes," Atiernan said, returning his attention to the assembled daemons. "A witch caused us great harm once and seeks to harm us still. Only one person here has enough evidence stacked against her to fit such a crime." He inhaled, sensing that everything—his family's safety and the longevity of his pack—rested upon the next words to leave his mouth.

Spinning on his heel, he faced the culprit and extended an accusatory finger in their direction.

"I call upon you to witness the judgment of the witch Miranda and hear those who seek to bring proof of her crimes against us to light. Let the tribunal begin."

TWENTY-FIVE

While nowhere near an expert in intimate relationships with the opposite sex, Miranda knew enough to assume that being accused of treason was not a typical aspect of one. Still, Atiernan's words rang clearly in her mind, even as what seemed like hundreds of daemons turned their attention and ire in her direction.

Have faith. A surprisingly big ask when all was said and done. She'd applied the emotion so fervently to her coven for the past twenty-eight years. Though, in this case, failure meant potentially having her thoughts delved into by a thousands-year-old daemon warrior adept in the art of scrying.

For the time being, he didn't seem to be in a hurry to show off such a skill. He merely stood back, and Miranda realized that already—as if they had materialized from thin air—a group of eager daemons stood in the center of the room, presumably ready to present evidence of her sins.

One she vaguely recognized as the man she'd met alongside Atiernan the first day he let her out of the dungeon. Benjamin? He looked no older than she was, his dark hair arranged in a loose ponytail, his eyes narrowed in concentration.

"I saw the witch outside just before we noticed the outer perimeter had been breached," he explained, his voice rich and booming. "And who else was around when the sentinel entered our walls but her? The beast nearly killed her— proof that she was willing to die merely to harm even a few of us."

"Perhaps," Atiernan said, stepping forward. Apparently, in this iteration of a tribunal, he was to serve as judge, jury, and executioner—a thought that would have terrified her only a few days ago. Now? A thrill ran down her spine that she couldn't explain.

The man looked regal in this context, all eyes on him, their attention rapt. Regal and undeniably dangerous—her entire life rested in the palm of his hand.

And the daemon knew it.

He didn't look smug as he parsed over the accusations presented before him. No. In fact, he resembled a beast hunched over bleeding prey, unsure of where to bite first.

"You saw her open the door to the kitchens to let the sentinel in?" Atiernan asked.

The guard winced. "No, not directly, but she was the only one nearby when—"

"Bethaem was there as well," the daemon lord countered, pointing to the girl in question who stood near the back of the room beside her mother. "Perhaps she is the true culprit? Perhaps I should haul her here for judgment next?"

"Well, my lord… I?"

"And the breach in the outer wall, you noticed it when exactly?"

"Well, sir, I followed the witch as she raced from the manor to the grove. There, I spotted—"

"*You* followed her." Atiernan folded his arms, making the muscle coiled in his forearms strain against the sleeves of his black shirt. "A coy, cunning, sly witch allowing herself to be followed right to the scene of her own crime. That doesn't sound like the woman I know."

Miranda swallowed, finding herself riveted by the display. Slowly, Atiernan began to pace the center of the room, stroking his chin as he went.

"In fact, neither action sounds like Liva—"

At the mention of the name, an audible gasp ripped through the crowd. Contrary to his earlier statement, it seemed as though most of the daemons gathered here recognized that name and the evil it represented.

"And that doesn't sound like *you*, Ben," Atiernan went on. "You were never quick to judgment. Never one to rush to any conclusion without ample evidence and reason. You are not reckless. I know you," the leader continued, advancing on the man in question. "Hells below, I practically raised you. For you to be this sure, you must have proof—a basis that you believe in enough to stake your reputation on it. If you didn't see Miranda commit these crimes, you must know someone who did. Someone whose word you trust implicitly. Who told you?"

Benjamin sputtered. "I… My lord, I…"

"Who?" Atiernan growled, lowering his hands by his sides. "Though I think I can guess. I believe we might need to add another defendant to this trial."

"I agree," a voice pitched in, one surprisingly close to Miranda.

She turned to find Peony leaning against the desk beside her, her lips fixed in a cold grin. "It's a good thing I already thought to secure the woman in question. Give the order now, Atiernan, to bring her in."

The daemon lord shouted a command that was heeded within seconds. Appearing in the doorway, shouldered by two armed guards, was a woman Miranda only vaguely recognized.

She was tall, achingly beautiful, wearing a low-cut ruby gown that showed off most of her ample body. Flashing green eyes took in the room fearfully, and Miranda realized another detail that caught her off guard. This woman wasn't a witch or a daemon.

She was mortal.

"Sanna," Atiernan said, his tone ice. "Was it you who claimed to see the witch Miranda in the act of letting the sentinel inside the manor and creating the breach in the outer wall?"

The woman seemed to diminish beneath the scrutiny as the guards herded her to the center of the room to stand beside Benjamin.

"My lord," she said in a trembling voice. "I don't understand—"

"Answer the question." Atiernan stood tall, casting a shadow that made something inside Miranda quiver in recognition. He may have spent centuries atoning for his past sins, but what he'd told her once remained the truth—he was still that man, capable of ruthless leadership, fearsome to behold. "Did you see those crimes take place or not?"

"What word does a mortal have in this court?" Benjamin asked. "I am the one who—"

"You made the charges because that is how Liva works," Atiernan said over him. "By using others to spread chaos and deception. By driving a wedge between my closest guard and me, she would do far more than sow terror with the sentinel attacks. Now, answer the question, woman—" He turned the full brunt of his stare on Sanna, who cowered in response. "Did you see those acts take place?"

"Y-Yes," the woman said. "The witch is cunning, my lord. But I saw her—"

"And you didn't think to come to your lord directly?" Peony asked, her eyes steely behind the lenses of her glasses. "You let such a monster roam our halls unattended?"

"My lord, I could never get an audience with you," Sanna said, her large eyes welling with tears. "Please. I don't understand—"

"You could never get an audience with me," Atiernan echoed. "Because I do not feed from anyone, not even the willing humans kept here. A practice I have upheld for years, long enough for word to reach Liva and her spies. So, if she were to plant a snake in my midst, who better than a sensual mortal who would appeal to every man but me?"

Miranda couldn't ignore a tiny, selfish bit of pride in knowing Atiernan had never been with the woman—not that it made it any easier to witness this mess unfold. What was he up to? Humiliating a conniving human, while satisfying, couldn't be his sole aim.

"Watch," Peony murmured into her ear as if sensing her doubt. "Liva knows Atiernan, surely, but he knows her in return. Don't underestimate him now."

Underestimate? Was that what she'd been doing?

Miranda wasn't sure. As her gaze returned to the daemon lord, she had to admit that there was a side to him she had yet to discover in full.

The commanding general skilled in the art of war.

"A lone human who consorts with daemons afraid of a witch? There were other ways to make your accusations known, if they had any merit to them."

"My lord, I don't… Benjamin, please." The woman turned to the man beside her. "Please. I don't understand what's going on."

The soldier winced. "My lord."

"He'll kill all of us over that woman," Sanna cried. "We've all seen it! We've seen the way he coddles her, protects her. He should be protecting us."

A murmur ran through the crowd as the daemons discussed the statement amongst themselves.

"Not her," Sanna went on. "Please, he will use me as a way to appease this woman. This outsider. He should be banishing her from here for all our sakes!"

The murmurs grew louder, and Miranda was alarmed to realize that she couldn't guess the gist of the prevailing senti-ment. Many daemons seemed unconvinced, but a few nodded in agreement.

"Please! I am not the culprit here! This man isn't fit to lead you—"

"That is enough," a voice rang out, resonating authority—but it wasn't Atiernan's. Peony came around the desk, her head cocked skeptically. "Enough chattering and reveal yourself, spy," she snarled in a tone Miranda had never heard her utilize. "Now. Before sheer boredom kills us all before your mistress can."

Sanna sank to her knees, sobbing openly. "I am no spy," she wailed. "Benjamin, please…"

The guard flinched toward her, his gaze conflicted. "My lord, I don't understand. What is the meaning of this?"

"The meaning is simple," Atiernan replied, unmoved by the emotional display. "Liva would be far too cowardly to use a witch as her spy, or even a daemon. Daemons are useful tools, but only when controlled by their weaknesses, hunger, or lust. Witches, on the other hand? How that race has foiled her from the very beginning. They can't be so easily controlled , for they are just as greedy as she is. At her core, Liva is a coward, so fearful of the women she empowered and let thrive. She's been careful until now, very careful, letting her spy worm her way into the very heart of my fortress undetected. But at the presence of another witch, she became afraid and reacted impulsively."

Confusion spread through the crowd like wildfire, and Miranda counted herself among them.

"I don't understand," she said, hating how weak her voice sounded. She barely spoke louder than a whisper, yet Atiernan cocked his head in her direction, easily picking up every word.

"We believe that I was the target of the beast, but that wasn't the case in the most recent attack, was it?" He shook his head, his gaze fixed on the wailing Sanna. "No. With a beast so near, and the witch unguarded, you and your mistress took a risk to not only get rid of your main threat, but, hopefully, trigger a bloodlust I've kept restrained for all these years. You knew my scent would be on the witch, making her a tempting target to any sentinel. While I remain your main target, you wouldn't have minded, pardon the pun, killing two birds with one stone."

Miranda felt her eyes widen as she suddenly understood. Liva's goal hadn't been to harm Atiernan with that attack or even a wayward daemon. Just her.

"She would never admit it, but this witch has been a thorn in her side for nearly thirty years, thwarting her grand schemes and undermining her worst expectations. This witch isn't like the ilk she came from. She isn't greedy, and she isn't selfish. She didn't hesitate to place herself in harm's way to save another, and she didn't hesitate to sacrifice her life to keep us safe when faced with Liva herself. What do you say to that, spy?"

Sanna seemed barely able to breathe, let alone speak, in between her gasping sobs. With difficulty, she regained control of her breathing, her eyes fearful. "I say…"

Suddenly, she lurched to her feet and snatched a knife from the sheath at Benjamin's side. With an inhuman skill, she freed the blade and threw it.

Right in Miranda's direction.

In the back of her mind, she knew she could never be fast enough to evade such a weapon—not even aided by magic.

Luckily, a slim hand shot out before the blade could pierce her flesh.

"A pathetic attempt," Peony said, tossing the blade aside. "But I am sure your real aim was to distract us while you put whatever failsafe Liva intended for your ilk into effect. She would never let us question you, I am sure. Let me guess. A poison spell should you ever reveal yourself?"

"Oh, hush, you pathetic woman!" Sanna's eyes blazed as she shed her fearful image, carrying herself with sudden confidence, her chin in the air. "You are right, of course. I will die soon before you can even attempt to scry me, but know this—I come with a message." She smiled, her cackle a dangerously musical, beautiful sound. "Her death will be the beginning. The herald awaits her awakening, and no one can stand in the way of the incoming destruction."

With that, Sanna laughed—even as blood dripped from her eyes in lieu of tears. The scarlet liquid spilled from her mouth, ending her cackle in a violent gurgle as the woman fell to the floor, utterly silent.

"Well, that was dramatic," Peony remarked with a sigh. "I suggest we clean this up. Though you…" She turned to Miranda, her expression miles warmer than when she'd spoken to the mortal. "I hope you have no plans to return to your coven soon. It seems as if the fate of the world rests on you remaining here. Whether we like it or not."

Miranda didn't know what to say. For the first time, she noticed Marcus lurking near the doorway, his gaze watchful. She suspected both Peony and Atiernan had a hand in his presence here, but the meaning unnerved her.

This display hadn't been merely to unmask Liva's spy.

But to confirm their worst fear.

She was still destined to die, or Liva's grand scheme would never be able to unfold.

Which put a whole new meaning to the term protective custody.

TWENTY-SIX

Somehow, she managed to find some semblance of sleep wrapped in Atiernan's arms, but the moment the sun rose, she went alone into Peony's storeroom to retrieve the seedling of the light wood tree.

Already waiting for her at the entrance to the dungeon was Marcus.

"Are you sure about this?" he asked, displaying a rare hint of unease. Miranda suspected the question was primarily for show. The man seemed to have an unnerving insight into her emotions, and she sensed he knew her answer before she even voiced it.

"I think it's one way to at least try to beat Liva at her own game," she admitted.

One way beyond hiding in secret, hopeful her death might not trigger the start of the apocalypse. Doing so was a risk, of course—a bigger risk than sneaking out of bed while

Atiernan slept. His slumber alone revealed just how exhausted the warrior truly was beneath the valiant vigilance and bravado—therefore, she tried not to feel guilty for taking advantage of it.

In this case, she was willing to do whatever it took to take her fate into her own hands. Somehow.

"Let's go then," Marcus prompted. "After you."

Inside its cage, the sentinel was remarkably silent compared to their first meeting. It just watched them with those unsettling eyes, and Miranda questioned if she wasn't wasting a priceless artifact on a hopeless folly.

Then, the beast caught sight of her hand, and its nostrils flared as if it could sense what she held through smell alone.

"I know what you want," she said, unsure if the creature could understand her or not. Her descent into its mind seemed like an event from the distant past, and she could only vaguely recall snippets of emotion. Still, she hoped that her intentions were at least clear.

"I can give you a new tree to replant in your grove," she continued as the beast issued a low growl that she interpreted as only slightly threatening. "Plant it there, and it will protect your people for ages to come."

Or so she hoped.

"In return, you give me your word, and your honor. You will stop your people from coming here, and you will tell the truth about what happened."

Without caring whether or not the beast understood entirely, she explained the insidious nature behind the failing of their previous tree and the need to combat the old magic with a new one.

Once finished, the monster bared its fangs.

Strangely… The sight reassured her. Bits and pieces of its thought process returned—enough for her to recall that honor to the sentinels was like air to a mortal. They survived on it and without, would suffocate.

And yet, the hate and mistrust were still there. She could see it, lurking behind those fathomless red eyes. Still, one other aspect of sentinel culture returned, and—with only a quick, steadying breath—she took a step toward the bars of the cage.

"What are you doing?" Marcus called. "I can't heal your wounds if it harms you."

Yet, he didn't surge forward to stop her either. Not even as the sentinel lunged, throwing itself against the bars of the cage with a deafening clang and an ear-shattering roar.

Miranda felt her heart stop and braced for pain. Then, her ringing eardrums picked up a single note lurking within the animalistic snarl. A word?

Honor.

Trusting such a beast was probably more desperate than utilizing blood magic, but, in this instance, Miranda was willing to make an exception.

"Yes. Honor. I will heal your wounds," she said, holding the monster's stare. "I will give you a new light wood tree. In return, you give me your word."

The beast remained silent, but Miranda could sense an unspoken sentiment color the tension between them. A tenuous, fragile as hell truce?

She could only hope.

Hours after she returned to bed, she relished the comfort, too exhausted for guilt. There just wasn't room after Atiernan's passionate assault—her punishment for leaving once she explained what she'd done. All that remained was desperation for sleep and an unwillingness to move from her position curled against him.

"One day, you can go back to your coven with your dignity intact," Atiernan told her, his voice rumbling.

Miranda cracked an eyelid and found him staring down at her, his fingers parting through her hair. "You think I want to go back?"

He nodded. "In fact, I know you do. After everything they've done, some part of you probably still feels as though there is something in that damn coven worth salvaging."

And he was right. Beneath the hate, and the greed, the tenets of the witches remained pure. She couldn't doubt them—not even after everything she'd been through. While most of their teaching may have been corrupted by figures like Liva, at its core, the true spirit of what it meant to be a witch persisted. She could feel it, guiding her even now.

What had Marcus called it? *Meditation.* Perhaps, it simply was intuition.

"But, returning at all might just be a pathetic dream," she admitted out loud. "A daemon hoping to restore a coven of witches to grace?"

Especially one unknowingly named after the evilest witch alive? She couldn't even tell Atiernan that part of her ordeal. Maybe one day when she herself had come to terms with that moniker.

"Why not?" Atiernan countered.

She sighed. If only it were that simple.

She wouldn't be returning any time soon. But when? That date seemed elusive, and she wasn't in a hurry to answer it.

She figured this question had been weighing on her mind for days, only to find a voice now.

"I can't go back. Not until I'm strong enough to defeat Liva at her own game."

Though it wasn't like there were many options available to her otherwise.

"I could go with Marcus to the mortal realm." She still needed to devise a spell to help him return home, anyway. Though, merely to needle the warrior beside her, she added, "I'm sure he will protect me—"

"You will stay here," Atiernan said. "Not as a captive."

"Just as a lover you can't allow out of your sight," she said tiredly.

"I don't see a damn thing wrong with that," he replied, his voice low. "Do you?"

She mulled over the possibility, unwilling to answer just yet. Instead, she relished his nearness. For now, it was enough to have the space to think without duty or shame weighing her down.

There would be time to make a choice later.

First, she needed to recover—a task that Atiernan seemed more than willing to assist her in doing.

His hands were gentle as he splayed his fingers along her upper back, working through the stiff, sore muscle. The ministrations lulled her into a false sense of security—she barely noticed when his hands began to dangerously inch lower.

"You can worry about starting the apocalypse later," he said.

"And Marcus and the sister he believes to be the harbinger," she added. Atiernan had divulged that information right after the debacle with Sanna. "She will need protection as well."

"Later," the daemon lord said dismissively. "For now, you only need rest and for your every whim to be tended to."

She opened both eyes in time to watch his hands ghost over her breasts. "By you, I assume?"

"Who else?" he countered. "You are mine, witch. Whether you like it or not."

~ The Daemon Blade Series continues with Logan's story in Daemon's Blade. ~

A WORD FROM THE AUTHOR

Hey there!

Thank you so much for reading! If you enjoyed the story, please leave a review and recommend the book to any friend you think would love this twisted world. You'd have my eternal gratitude. Even a short sentence goes a long way!

Then, come join the rest of us dark romance lovers in my Facebook Group where you can get snippets, sneak peeks of upcoming books and even help vote on aspects of future novels.

Come to the dark side:
https://www.facebook.com/groups/lanasbeautifulmonsters/

WANT MORE STUFF TO READ?
Join my newsletter and get a **free book**! Plus, you get to stay updated with any new releases, random giveaways and exclusive sneak peeks!
https://www.lanaskybooks.com/newsletter

Other Novels: https://lanaskybooks.com/

FREE BOOK - JOIN MY NEWSLETTER

DARK, TWISTED ROMANCE

Join my newsletter and get a **free book**! Plus, you get to stay updated with any new releases, random giveaways and exclusive sneak peeks!

https://www.lanaskybooks.com/newsletter

ABOUT THE AUTHOR

Lana Sky is a reclusive writer in the United States who spends most of her time daydreaming about complex male characters and parenting her Cockapoo Joey. She writes dark, twisted romance across several genres. Her titles include everything from mafia romance to vampires.

facebook.com/AuthorLanaSky

twitter.com/lanasky101

amazon.com/author/lanasky

pinterest.com/lanasky101

goodreads.com/lanasky

instagram.com/lanasky101

bookbub.com/authors/lana-sky

tiktok.com/@author_lana_sky

ALSO BY LANA SKY

For more titles by Lana Sky, please visit:

https://www.lanaskybooks.com